The Plant That Ate Dirty Socks Goes Up In Space

Nancy McArthur

AN AVON CAMELOT BOOK

AVON BOOKS, INC.
1350 Avenue of the Americas
New York, New York 10019

Copyright © 1995 by Nancy McArthur
Published by arrangement with the author
Library of Congress Catalog Card Number: 94-96869
ISBN: 0-380-77664-2
RL: 4.9
www.avonbooks.com

First Avon Camelot Printing: August 1995

CAMELOT TRADEMARK REG. U.S. PAT. OFF. AND IN OTHER COUNTRIES, MARCA REGISTRADA, HECHO EN U.S.A.

Printed in the U.S.A.

OPM 10 9 8 7 6 5 4

To Barbara McArthur,
who suggested that the plants go into space

Special thanks to: principal Rick Hayman and librarian Mary Kay Hahn of Edison Elementary School, Willoughby, Ohio, who gave me detailed information about their events with astronaut Greg Harbaugh, who attended Edison as a child; June Bahan-Szucs; Jo Crabtree; Nick Stiner-Riley; Emma Stiner-Riley; Margaret Stiner; Susan McArthur; John McArthur; the Buckeye Book Fair; and Jackie Harris.

Other Avon Camelot Books by
Nancy McArthur

THE PLANT THAT ATE DIRTY SOCKS
THE RETURN OF THE PLANT THAT ATE DIRTY SOCKS
THE ESCAPE OF THE PLANT THAT ATE DIRTY SOCKS
THE SECRET OF THE PLANT THAT ATE DIRTY SOCKS
MORE ADVENTURES OF THE PLANT THAT ATE DIRTY SOCKS
THE MYSTERY OF THE PLANT THAT ATE DIRTY SOCKS

Coming Soon

THE PLANT THAT ATE DIRTY SOCKS GETS A GIRLFRIEND

NANCY McARTHUR's first published writing was in her school newspaper. She starts writing a book with "a very messy rough draft. Then I revise two or three times." This is the sixth book about Michael and Norman and their amazing plants. The eighth one will be published in mid-1997. Ms. McArthur lives in Berea, Ohio, a suburb of Cleveland. She also teaches journalism part-time at Baldwin-Wallace College and speaks to school groups. She has a lot of plants, but none of them has eaten anything—so far

Chapter 1

"Bugs?" mumbled Dad from deep in his pillow. "You don't need me for that. It's the middle of the night. Just swat 'em and go back to bed."

Michael tugged on his father's arm again. So he wouldn't wake Mom on the other side of the bed, he whispered, "There's too many to swat by myself. You have to get up."

Dad was not interested in getting up to squash bugs. He mumbled, "Wake up Norman. You two can handle it."

"I already woke him up. He took one look and ran out of the room."

Dad groaned and sat up. "How did you get bugs in there? Did you leave some old snacks under your bed? Remember you promised you'd stop being messy. That was part of our deal to let you keep your plant."

1

Michael replied, "This is *not* my fault. It's an experiment that got messed up."

Mom murmured, "What's going on? Another plant uproar?"

Dad said, "It's not the plants this time. Just a few bugs in the boys' room. Go back to sleep."

"Bugs?" exclaimed Mom, sitting up suddenly.

Dad assured her, "I'll take care of it." She plopped back down on her pillow.

Michael picked up Dad's sneakers. "You better put these on," he said.

"Good thinking," said Dad. "We don't want to stomp bugs with bare feet." They went into the hall. Michael and his younger brother Norman, the neatness nut and expert pest, shared their room with their giant sock-eating pet plants.

Their door was usually left slightly open at night to let in a little light from the hall. But Michael had closed it when he went to get Dad. Now, slowly, he opened it. He stuck his head inside to scout the situation. Dad put his head in above Michael's.

The lights were on. Standing next to Michael's bed was his six-foot-tall plant, Stanley. Next to Norman's bed was his plant, Fluffy, a few inches shorter. Norman was not there.

The plants' large pots were firmly fastened to skateboards to make them easy to move around. Stanley and Fluffy had also learned to roll around on their own by pulling with their vines. Now they appeared to be dancing wildly. They wiggled and wriggled as if they were being tickled. Their vines swatted at unseen bugs. Putting vines in and out and shaking them all about, they looked as if they were doing the dance that Norman had taught them—the hokey-pokey.

Dad and Michael stepped in and closed the door. Dad noticed that the plain walls appeared to have been redecorated with dotted wallpaper. But the dots were moving.

"They're on the walls!" exclaimed Dad.

"And the floor," added Michael. "And the furniture. And Stanley and Fluffy."

Stepping on bugs wherever he walked, Dad said sternly, "I want an explanation of how these got in here." Michael was baffled about what to say. After he and Norman had seen a fossil of a prehistoric plant like theirs that had eaten a bug, Norman had secretly ordered the bugs by mail. He wanted to see if Fluffy and Stanley would eat them. Then they might not eat so many socks. Dad was always complaining about having to spend so much money on socks for plant food.

Every night the boys put out six dirty socks for Stanley and five clean ones for Fluffy. The plants lifted them with vines to a few of their leaves that were rolled up like ice cream cones. They sucked them in with a loud "Schlurrp!" Then they burped. Fluffy also made a noise that sounded like "Ex!" because Norman had tried to teach his plant to say "Excuse me."

Michael had done some weird experiments of his own to try to cut down on the plants' big appetites. So he understood what Norman had been trying to do. For once, he was not eager to rat on his little brother.

Dad said, "First, we have to find Norman to make sure he's all right."

But the mystery of the missing Norman was solved immediately. They heard the toilet flush and the bathroom door open. Norman came in carrying his Super Splasher Water Blaster. It was fully loaded with several quarts.

He said casually, "Oh, hi, Dad," as if a room full of bugs in the middle of the night was nothing unusual.

Dad demanded, "What do you think you're doing with that thing?"

"I'm going to take Fluffy out in the backyard and water blast the bugs off him so they'll fall on the grass. Then the bugs can run away and eat bad bugs and live happily ever after in the yard." Dad looked dumbfounded, so Norman explained, "These are good bugs that eat bad bugs that eat plants."

Dad shook his head in disbelief. "Put some

shoes on," he instructed Norman as he squashed a few crawling invaders with his foot.

Norman shrieked, "Don't kill them! They're good bugs, and they cost a lot of money!"

"You bought these?" Dad asked. "On purpose? You actually bought bugs? With what? Your allowance money?"

"I saved up," said Norman, stuffing his bare feet into sneakers. "I saw a bugs ad in a garden magazine."

Michael came to his brother's defense. "It was just an experiment. And when we opened the box, the bugs weren't moving."

Norman explained, "I thought they were asleep, but Michael said they were dead. See?" he told Michael. "I told you so! They *were* just asleep!"

"So you were right," said Michael. "Big deal!" He told Dad, "But they looked dead. We put some on Stanley and Fluffy to see if they might eat them anyway. But they weren't interested. So Norman put the box of bugs under his bed and we went to sleep. The next thing I knew, Stanley woke me up when he swatted a bug that was walking across my nose. When I turned on the light, there were bugs on the wall and Stanley and Fluffy were wiggling like crazy. I woke Norman up, and he panicked and ran out."

"I didn't panic," said Norman huffily. "I had to go to the bathroom."

"You never ran for the bathroom that fast before," said Michael.

Dad asked Norman, "Why didn't you tell me about this?"

"We just did," replied Norman.

"I mean that you wanted to do this experiment."

"It was supposed to be a surprise," said Norman, looking defeated. He stared at the floor, his chin down on his chest, his shoulders slumped. Fluffy stopped wiggling long enough to gently ruffle Norman's hair with one vine and pat him on the back with another.

"It's a surprise all right," said Dad. He put an arm around Norman. "I know you didn't mean to do anything wrong," he told him. "You're going to have to be grounded for a few days. And no more surprise experiments. Promise?"

"I promise," said Norman, starting to look cheered up. He swatted at his left arm. He pulled up his pajama sleeve and saw a squashed bug. "Oops," he said. He brushed it off into the wastebasket.

"We still got a lot left," he said.

"Hundreds," said Michael.

Dad said, "We have to figure how to get them out of here. Preferably before your mother wakes up. If it's all over before breakfast and we tell her about it then, she'll think it's funny. But if she sees this, she's not going to be happy, to put it mildly."

Michael swatted a couple of bugs on the wall with a rolled-up magazine. That left tiny dark splotches of bug juice on the white wall. "I guess swatting's not going to work too good," he concluded.

"No," said Dad. "Bug juice-spotted walls will not catch on as a new style of interior decorating."

"You can't see the spots on the dark rug," observed Michael. "We can knock 'em all off onto the floor and squash 'em there!"

"Don't squash them!" squealed Norman.

"Keep your voice down," warned Dad.

Norman whispered, "We can blow the ones on the walls off with Mom's hair dryer."

Dad said, "Blow them off to where? We'd just wind up with a room full of blow-dried bugs."

Norman said, "We can blow them out the window."

"No," said Dad. "The roar of the dryer would wake her up."

Michael said, "Then I guess the vacuum cleaner wouldn't work either."

"Right," agreed Dad. "Sucking them up would be better than blowing them around, but we need a quiet method. Norman, go get the broom and dustpan. We'll sweep them off the walls." Norman ran down the hall to the kitchen.

Michael looked closely at his bed before he sat down on it. He didn't want bug juice on his pajamas. Stanley was standing more calmly now, just twitching a vine here and there. He must have shaken off the bugs that had been bothering him. Fluffy was still poking vines at his main stalk as if he had an itch that was moving around.

When Norman returned, Dad took the broom and told Michael to hold the dustpan. With long careful sweeps of the broom, the bugs were pushed or fell into the dustpan. Some clung to the broom.

Holding the first dustpanful, Michael said, "Now what? Where do we put them?"

"Out the window," said Norman. "They can live happily ever after in the backyard." He struggled to open the window.

Dad said, "This is not a bug fairy tale, but I guess that's the shortest way to get them out of the house."

"It *could* be a bug fairy tale," said Norman. "Remember that story about the frog that turned into a princess or a prince—or something like that? I forget exactly. There could be a bug that turns into a prince or princess."

Michael said, "But somebody had to kiss the

frog to turn it into a person. If you want to kiss a bunch of bugs to see if you can find a princess, go right ahead."

Norman gave him a dirty look and shut up for a while, which is what Michael had hoped for.

They worked on silently. Norman got a piece of cardboard and brushed bugs off the furniture onto it. Then he held the cardboard out the window and gently brushed the bugs off into the dark.

Michael stuck his head out the window and said, "Good night, princesses." Norman bonked him with the piece of cardboard, but he ignored that.

They took turns at the window, Michael unloading the dustpan, Norman with his cardboard, and Dad flicking clinging bugs off the broom.

Finally, Dad said, "I think we've got most of them. The ones left seem to be mostly on the rug."

The door swung slowly open. Standing there in her purple robe, pink pajamas, and bare feet was Mom.

Chapter 2

"What's going on?" asked Mom. Before anyone could speak up to stop her, she stepped on several bugs as she walked across the rug.

"Look out!" said Norman.

"What?" she said, stopping in the middle of the room.

"Bugs," said Dad.

"Where?" she asked, glancing around.

"Stuck to your feet," said Michael. Mom appeared to go straight up in the air. She leaped onto Norman's bed.

"This is totally disgusting," she said. She sat down cross-legged to inspect the bottoms of her feet. "There are no bugs stuck here," she announced.

Norman came over to look and picked some squashed bugs off his top blanket. "They fell off when you jumped on my bed," he said. He threw them out the window.

Michael looked at her feet. "Just a little bug juice," he told her.

"Ugh," said Mom. "Somebody go get me some shoes, so I can get out of here."

"Don't you want to know what happened?" asked Dad.

"No. Whatever it was, the plants must have started it. We've had nothing but uproars since the boys grew them. But we're stuck with them because Fluffy saved Norman from falling off a cliff and we promised they could stay, trouble or no trouble. So as long as you've got the problem under control, I don't care what happened. I just want to get out of here without getting any more bug juice on my feet. My feet had enough trouble yesterday. At Shawn and Belinda Smith's wedding, when my new shoes were killing me and I slipped them off under the table at the reception, I wound up with a shoe full of chocolate syrup."

"That wasn't my fault," said Norman.

"I know," said Mom. "I'm not blaming you. It was Mrs. Smith's idea to have you serve the chocolate syrup with your Water Blaster. Why she thinks things like that are cute, I'll never know. Right now all I want is to put my feet back in my own bed and sleep late all Sunday morning."

Norman asked, "Aren't you going to get up and make breakfast?"

Mom replied, "You all know where the juice and milk and cereal are." Michael came back with her sneakers. She clumped out of the room with untied shoelaces flapping, squashing a few more bugs on the way.

Dad said, "Since she already woke up, Michael, go get the vacuum cleaner."

The vacuum made short work of the remaining bugs, at least all those they could find. But when Norman tried to use the hose attachment to get a few left on Fluffy, the plant flattened himself against the wall trying to get away. Stanley reached a vine over and flicked the switch off. Norman stroked Fluffy's leaves to calm him down and gave him a hug. Fluffy hugged him back.

Dad opened the vacuum cleaner and took out the dirt collection bag that now also held bugs.

"Take this outside to the garbage can," he told Michael. "I don't want to take a chance on leaving it in the kitchen wastebasket. If any bugs in there are still alive, we don't want them getting out in the house."

"I'll do it," said Norman, grabbing the dirt bag. He went out the back door. Over the garage roof, he could see the sky starting to get light. But he did not put the bag into the garbage can. He put it down next to the can and opened the bag. That way any bugs left alive could crawl out to live happily ever after in the yard.

Because it was Sunday, the whole family went back to bed and slept late. Norman woke first as usual and wheeled Fluffy into the kitchen to keep him company. He fixed himself a bowl of his favorite cereal, Tummy Yummy Globsters. He neatly sliced circles of banana and spaced them evenly around his bowl.

While he ate and talked to Fluffy, he noticed a bug climbing down the plant's skateboard wheels. Norman scooped it up with a napkin and put it out the back door. Michael straggled in, looking sleepy with his hair rumpled every which way. He poured his favorite cereal, Super Gooper Bunch-O-Crunch, sloppily into his bowl. Flakes drifted over the sides.

Dad came in and mumbled, "Morning." He started the coffee maker and went to the front door to get the newspaper. He poured them all some juice and sat down.

Michael asked him, "Do you think we got them all?"

"If we didn't," replied Dad, "we can deal with the leftovers one by one. A couple bugs here and there won't be a problem." He started reading the paper.

Norman decided that after such a hard night, Fluffy needed cheering up. So he started singing

13

"Oh, Susannah," waving his spoon in time to the song.

To Michael, Norman's off-key singing sounded about as musical as an aluminum lawn chair being dragged across a concrete driveway.

"Your singing is making me nauseous," he said.

Dad said more tactfully, "Eat now. Sing later."

"I already ate," said Norman.

"Sing later anyway," said Dad. Norman looked annoyed.

While Dad was behind the newspaper and Norman turned away to look at Fluffy, Michael flicked a piece of cereal at his brother. The first one missed. The second one hit Norman's ear. He jumped.

"What was that?"

"A bug princess trying to kiss you," said Michael.

Norman saw the flakes on the floor. "He's throwing Super Goopers at me!" he whined.

"Stop it!" commanded Dad. "Go pick up what you threw. And quit playing with your food." He went on reading. "Hey, listen to this! Another space shuttle's going up soon, and one of the astronauts on the crew used to live here. His name's Mark Fortunato. He went to Edison Elementary through sixth grade before his family moved away."

"Our school!" exclaimed Michael.

Dad showed them the page with the astronaut's picture.

"Cool," said Norman.

"Awesome," said Michael.

Mom came in as they were clustered around the paper. "Morning," she said. "What's so interesting?" They told her about the astronaut who had gone to their school.

She asked, "What are they going to do on the flight? Put up another satellite or do space walks?"

Dad read, "They're taking up Spacelab to do chemical, animal, and plant experiments in microgravity."

Michael asked, "What kind of plant experiments?"

"The article doesn't say."

Norman noticed another bug strolling by. He gave it a ride to the back door.

"What was that?" asked Mom. Norman shrugged. "Not another one of those bugs," she said. Norman nodded.

Dad said, "I'm sure we got all of them, except maybe one or two."

"Then," said Mom, "you guys can be in charge of bug patrol—every day, just in case."

Chapter 3

Monday morning the school was buzzing about the news of the astronaut who had gone there. The principal, Mr. Leedy, included it in the morning announcements on the PA in case anybody had missed it in the newspaper or on TV on Sunday. He said the school would plan something special to celebrate.

After lunch, Michael's teacher, Mrs. Black, told her class that the teachers had come up with a lot of great ideas while they ate in the teachers' lounge.

"Like what?" asked Chad Palmer.

"Wait and see," said Mrs. Black, smiling. "Some of them are really big ideas. First, we want to find out if we can actually do them."

Michael asked, "Was Mark Fortunato ever in your room?"

"No, he went here more than twenty years ago. No one teaching here now was here then."

Every day her students pestered her to find out what was going on. She just smiled and said, "Be patient. We'll know soon."

Mr. Leedy announced that he had talked to some retired teachers who remembered Mark. They said he had been outstanding in math and science and sports.

On Friday, as Michael walked past the open doors of the gym, he saw the custodian, Mr. Jones, rolling out a long metal tape measure and marking the floor with chalk. Mr. Leedy was walking around inside the space Mr. Jones had marked off.

"I think this will leave enough room to have the gym classes around it, don't you?" asked Mr. Leedy.

"Don't ask me," replied Mr. Jones. "Ask the gym teacher." He stood back, as if he were picturing what was going to go in the measured-off space. "If we go ahead with this," he added, "it's going to be great."

"We'll know this afternoon," said Mr. Leedy. "The parents' organization is letting me know whether they'll provide some of the money and how many hours they'd be willing to volunteer."

What were they up to? Michael wondered as he went on down the hall. What was this thing in the gym going to be? Probably some kind of science exhibit about space flights. That would be interesting. And any laps they had to run in gym class would be shorter. That would be good, too.

When he got to his desk, he told Chad Palmer, Jason Greensmith, and Brad Chan. Pat Jenkins came over from the other side of the room to ask what he had told the boys. Michael thought Pat must have radar ears because she seemed to overhear everybody. Just then Mrs. Black came in, so they asked her what was going on in the gym.

She smiled and said, "You'll all find out today before school is out. Now settle down. We have a lot to do today."

After lunch, Mr. Leedy came to the door of their room and beckoned to Mrs. Black to come out in the hall. The kids could hear them whispering but couldn't make out what they said.

Michael whispered to Pat, "Can you hear what they're saying?"

Pat said, "Something about space flight in the gym."

"It's an exhibit," said Michael.

Mrs. Black came back in. "Here's the good news," she announced. "When the space shuttle goes up, we're going to do a mock space flight right here at school. Of course, we won't be going anywhere, except in our imaginations. But it'll be fun, and we'll learn a lot."

"What about the gym?" asked Pat.

"That's the best part," said Mrs. Black. "Mr. Jones is going to build a copy of the shuttle's flight deck and crew deck in the gym so you can get in and feel like you're in the real ones.

"And that's not all," she continued. "The cafeteria will serve space food like the astronauts eat. Since every space crew has a special patch to put on their outfits, we'll have a contest to design one for our mission. Contest rules will be ready next week. And every class will set up science experiments to go on our flight. It's going to be thrilling! And maybe there'll be one more big event. But I can't talk about it until we find out if it's going to happen." She refused to give them even a hint about what the big event might be.

After school Michael and Norman arrived home at the same time. They both began talking at once, trying to be the first to tell Mom about the space flight.

"I already heard," she said. "The PTO president called and told me all about it. She asked me to be head of the space food committee."

Norman asked, "Do you know how to fix space food?"

"No," replied Mom, "but I guess I'm going to learn."

Norman, still eager to be the first to tell some-body the news, ran down the hall to tell Fluffy. Norman liked to talk to his plant. Fluffy was al-ways a good listener.

Michael got some orange juice from the refrig-erator and took a couple of oatmeal raisin cookies from the cookie jar.

The kitchen phone rang and Mom answered.

"Oh, hi, Susan," she said. "I was going to call you. How are things going?"

Michael said, "Is that Dr. Sparks?" Mom nod-ded. Dr. Susan Sparks was their botanist friend, a plant scientist. She had taken an interest in Stanley and Fluffy when her family and theirs had met on vacation in Florida. Then she had grown plants from the seeds they gave her. She was doing research with them, including training them to pick up trash. Michael thought she was probably calling about something new her plants were doing.

"Oh, really?" exclaimed Mom. "That's fabulous!"

Michael wondered what Dr. Sparks's small plants were up to now.

Mom told Michael, "You're not going to believe this! Go get on the bedroom phone to listen! And get Norman!"

Chapter 4

With the boys trying to grab the phone from each other, bumping their heads together so they could hear, Dr. Sparks repeated her good news: "NASA just okayed taking some of my little plants up on the next shuttle flight as an experiment!"

Michael asked, "What kind of experiment?"

"To see if they can perform tasks in space the way they can on Earth," she replied.

"Like what?"

"Pick up trash, the way we've got them doing it at our research center. Only in space the trash doesn't sit still on the floor. It floats around. In space everything floats around, even people. So this will be very difficult."

Norman said, "Floating people should pick up their own trash. Or put their stuff away so they don't make a mess in the first place."

"Yeah," said Michael scornfully. "You should get a job giving the astronauts neatness lessons."

Mom asked, "Susan, how did all this come about? Did NASA call you or did you call them?"

Dr. Sparks replied, "I sent in a proposal for this months ago. I was trying to think of other uses for our plants. It occurred to me that if my trash training worked, the plants would be very valuable tools in future space flights. There's already been research to see how plants absorb air pollution in closed spaces and help maintain a healthy atmosphere. They might do this when humans are in space for a long time. If plants like ours could also do work in space, they could be even more useful—even on unmanned space missions.

"So an experiment was planned to take up some good-sized plants, ones proven good at cleaning the air. But there were some problems with this. When the committee heard that my plants could also do tasks, they considered it and today they gave me a go-ahead!

"One other thing that appealed to the committee is that these plants are survivors of ones that lived in dinosaur times. They like the idea of plants from prehistory flying into the future of space."

Norman asked, "But won't the plants float around too?"

"Yes," replied Dr. Sparks, "but they can be fastened down."

Michael asked, "But what will they eat in space?"

"The astronauts' dirty socks," she said. "They change their clothes every two days, including socks, and stow the dirty ones in sealed plastic bags in trash compartments. That'll be the food supply. So this'll be real recycling: the plants absorb carbon dioxide breathed out by the astronauts and other chemicals in the air. They give off oxygen, eat the socks, and clean up the trash. It's perfect! *If* it works as planned."

Norman asked, "I want to see them do this. Is this gonna be on TV?"

"Yes, there's a satellite channel where you can watch what's happening on shuttle flights. I'll find out where in your town you can watch it."

"Cool!" said Norman.

Michael asked, "How many of your little plants are going?"

"Four," said Dr. Sparks. "I'm going to train twenty. Then at the last minute, I'll pick my four best workers. While they're up in space, we'll do the same experiments with the rest of the plants on Earth. Experiments are run in both places at the same time to compare the results. And if there are any problems with the ones in space, scientists use the ones on Earth to figure out what to do."

"This is really exciting," said Mom.

"Yes," said Dr. Sparks. "If it works, who knows what it might lead to in the future? Perhaps plants could work on flights that are going to be gone for years. Maybe even plants in their own space suits, doing walks out of spaceships to pick up some of the trash that's orbiting our planet."

Norman asked, "There's trash in space? How can that be?"

Dr. Sparks replied, "About three and a half thousand pieces of all sizes are going around and around Earth. I read an article about it."

"Astronauts threw trash out in space?" said Norman. He was finding this hard to believe.

"Not exactly," said Dr. Sparks. "They're mostly things that got left behind because it was easier to leave them there than bring them back."

Norman said indignantly, "Only neat people should be allowed to be astronauts! *They* wouldn't leave junk in space. They'd pick it up and bring it back in garbage bags and recycle it!"

"It's not that simple," said Dr. Sparks. "This junk isn't cans and bottles and plastic jugs. It's large and small things, used-up equipment, and little broken pieces of metal and plastic. You couldn't bring that stuff back in garbage bags."

24

Norman said, "They could invent some really big garbage bags."

"Maybe some day," said Dr. Sparks, "somebody will figure out how to clean it up. Maybe when you grow up you can work on that."

Mom asked, "Do you get to go to Florida for the shuttle launch?"

"I don't know all the details yet. Listen, I've got to get off the phone and back to work here. I just wanted to tell you the good news right away."

"Congratulations," said Mom. "And keep us posted."

After they all hung up, Michael went back to his cookies, but he felt too excited to eat.

When Dad got home, the boys surrounded him, both talking at once, to tell him Dr. Sparks's news.

Dad said, "This is going to be some space flight with those plants on board. I hope the astronauts have better luck keeping them under control than we do with Fluffy and Stanley."

Mom said, "The plants Susan's been training don't pull themselves around on skateboards or do the hokey-pokey. All they do is pick up trash and drop it in cans and behave themselves. They'll probably do a very good job in space. And," she joked, "if they do well, maybe we can get Stanley and Fluffy jobs in space, for one of the longer missions."

The boys did not think that was funny, but Dad laughed.

Then Michael and Norman told him about the space flight at school.

"That'll be very educational," said Dad, "and it sounds like fun."

Mom said, "I'm glad you think that, because I told the PTO chairman you'd help on the space-ship building committee. I'm in charge of the space food committee."

"Oh, great," said Dad. "First you got us all mixed up in helping with Shawn and Belinda's wedding. And now this."

"It'll be fun," said Norman.

Dad said, "I'm afraid to ask what we're having for dinner. I hope it's Earth food."

Chapter 5

The whole school got busy planning the mock space flight. Mr. Leedy started calling the school office "Mission Control." A sign with a countdown to the big day was posted inside the front door. "T minus 40," said the sign on the first day. The T stood for takeoff. The number of days to go was changed every morning.

Michael remarked to his friend Chad, "Wouldn't it be funny if the whole building really took off?"

"Yeah," replied Chad, chuckling. "But Mr. Leedy would be running after us, yelling, 'Come back here with that building!'"

Michael and Norman told their teachers and a lot of kids about relatives of their plants going up on the shuttle. When Mr. Leedy heard about it, he asked Michael to ask their parents if they could bring their plants to school for the mock flight.

Also posted in the hall were interesting space facts. Classes had to take turns finding the facts and typing them into a computer to print them out in big letters. Norman's class drew eighth turn for this job. Michael's drew twelfth turn.

Jason Greensmith complained, "All the good facts will be taken before we get to do it."

"Don't worry," said Mrs. Black. "There are more than enough interesting space facts to go around. We won't run out."

All the books and videos about space flights got checked out of the school and public libraries. The librarians had to start waiting lists. The teachers got packets of information from NASA with classroom activities to do.

Kids collected space facts in their notebooks and on scraps of paper. Because there were many brothers and sisters in different grades, students tried to keep their facts secret from anyone in other classes so those who had earlier turns could not use them first. Some made up secret codes to write their facts in.

One evening, Michael caught Norman snooping in his notebook. "Ha, ha!" Michael gloated. "My space facts aren't even in there. You'll never find them!"

"Yes, I will," said Norman. "I know where everything in this house is. You can't hide anything for long from me!"

Michael was sure Norman couldn't swipe his facts because he was keeping them on crumpled scraps of paper in his pockets. That worked fine until Michael forgot to clean out the pockets before his jeans went through the washer and dryer. His space facts turned into ragged lumps of unreadable pulp. He had to start over, writing down what he could remember and looking up the rest.

Michael was fascinated with facts about plants that had been in space. The first ones to go up were sunflowers. He found a picture of an experiment with mung beans sprouting in microgravity. Some of their roots got confused. They poked up out of the dirt instead of down into it. Part of Spacelab had equipment to investigate how plants react in space. Time-lapse video cameras recorded growth. Wheat and other food plants had been grown on the shuttle.

He read about a study of how indoor plants and the microbes in their potting soil remove harmful chemical air pollution. Michael already knew that plants take in carbon dioxide and give off oxygen, just the opposite of what humans do when they breathe. In a space station where humans worked and lived for a long time, the best pollution-removing plants might live there, too, to help keep the air healthy.

Scientists had put each plant into a sealed

Plexiglas chamber and injected a chemical to be tested. They measured air samples from the chamber as soon as they put the plants in, and again six hours and twenty-four hours later to find out how much of the chemical was left.

Some of plant names Michael recognized were English ivy, peace lily, golden pothos, bamboo palm, gerbera daisy, and sanseveria, also known as snake plant or mother-in-law's tongue.

Michael needed a big piece of paper to write down the information he found about the "Great National Science Project." About forty thousand schools had taken part. Twelve and a half million tomato seeds had been put into orbit in 1984 in a satellite containing fifty-seven experiments to see how a year's exposure to radiation in space would affect them. Another batch of seeds was set aside on Earth to compare later with the space-traveling ones.

But accidents and delays prevented bringing back the satellite until 1990. Then schools were sent packets of seeds that had spent six years in space and some that had been stored on Earth. Students planted the seeds and measured their germination times and growth.

Even though Michael had found wonderful facts, he was still curious about Norman's. He decided to snoop because Norman had done it first. He found no space facts in Norman's regular school notebook, so he kept looking every chance he got. Finally, he found a tiny green spiral notebook tucked into a sock at the bottom of Norman's neatly organized sock drawer. On the cover Norman had printed "Keep out!" Michael quickly memorized a couple of things and put the notebook back.

At dinner, when Dad was talking about his day at work, Michael suddenly remarked, "Frogs have gone up on the space shuttle."

Mom asked, "Are you sure you've got that right?"

"Yep," said Norman. "They really did." Then he glared at Michael suspiciously.

Dad said, "That's how they spend some of the taxpayers' hard-earned money? For frogs in space?"

Michael replied, "I think it was one of those experiments to see what microgravity does to different animals."

Norman said, "The first time a frog jumped in space, I bet it was surprised. It probably hit the ceiling."

Michael added, "They also sent up tadpoles and monkeys and rats and mice and newts and bugs and fish."

Now Norman was looking even more suspicious. But he just said, "It's a good thing they didn't send elephants up in space. If one of those jumped, it'd go crash, boing, bam, boom on all the walls. It might crash right through the spaceship and keep on going. Maybe to the moon."

Mom said, "I think plants in space make more sense than frogs in space. Plants can be really useful there, according to what Susan said."

"I like the idea of plant astronauts," agreed Michael.

Norman laughed and said, "They're plantronauts!"

"That's brilliant!" remarked Mom. "I'm going to tell Susan. She'll love it." Norman beamed with pride. Michael wished he'd thought of it.

Dad asked Mom, "How's the space food committee doing?"

"We haven't done anything yet," replied Mom. "We're meeting tomorrow. Mr. Leedy got us some material from NASA and a video of a shuttle flight we've been passing around. I got the video today. We can watch it after dinner."

Chapter 6

Norman called his best friend Bob from down the street to come over. They all gathered in the living room to watch the video.

"Are we going to have popcorn?" asked Bob.

"No," said Mom. "We just ate."

Bob added, "We always have popcorn at my house when we watch a video."

Norman asked, "Even after you just ate?"

"Sometimes," said Bob.

Mom pressed start on the remote control. The tape began with a shuttle launch from Kennedy Space Center at Cape Canaveral in Florida. The white orbiter that looked like an airplane stood nose-up, piggybacked on the huge orange fuel tank, pointed toward the sky. Two other tall white fuel tanks also clung to the big tank.

A voice counted down: "T minus thirty seconds and counting."

The whole family and Bob counted down along with launch control: "Five, four, three, two, one."

With a thundering roar, fuel under the rocket engines burned with an orange fire. Huge white clouds of steam billowed up. Slowly, the rocket started upward, lifting free of the launch pad, trailing a fiery tail of burning fuel pushing it toward space. Away it soared into the sky.

A shuttle pilot's voice explained, "It's the most bone-jarring, biggest roller coaster ride you could ever imagine."

Dad said, "I wouldn't go up on one of those things if they paid me a million dollars. I know they do everything they possibly can to be safe, but that's dangerous work."

The tape showed views of Earth from the orbiter's windows. An astronaut explained, "It only takes ninety minutes to fly all the way around the world. Every twenty-four hours we see sixteen sunrises and sixteen sunsets. The views are breathtaking."

The astronauts were shown working on experiments, exercising on a rowing machine and treadmill to stay in good shape, and sleeping in blue sleeping bags called sleep restraints. Since they were afloat in the air, they used built-in footholds to hook their feet under to stay put. As they floated, they pulled themselves from place to place with their arms, a little like the way Fluffy and Stanley did with their vines.

One astronaut explained, "Many people think there is no gravity here, but that's not true. The reason we float is that the orbiter and everything in it, including us, are free-falling in orbit around Earth. So there seems to be no gravity, and we feel weightless. In our training we practice this by going up in an airplane that makes steep, fast dives. For a moment, during those dives, we float just like in space. But it's hard on the stomach. We call that plane the Vomit Comet. Motion sickness often happens in space, too."

"Now I'm going to show you how we eat," said another astronaut. He took a small spoon and removed some food from a plastic bag. Then he let go of the spoon so it stayed in the air. He held his hands up, leaned forward, and put his mouth around the spoon.

"You have to eat carefully," he said, "so your food doesn't escape. Any sudden moves or even a little push can send it flying. Liquids can break up into tiny drops—except in microgravity they're shaped like perfectly round balls. And that's really a mess. We'd be bumping into them everywhere. Or accidentally inhale them up our noses. So we drink through special straws with clips in the middle to stop the flow—so drops can't escape. Everything's packaged carefully."

Another astronaut opened his mouth to catch a half-peeled banana sent spinning in his direction. Another lined up M&M's in a row in the air and snatched them up one by one with her mouth.

Michael pointed out, "They're playing with their food."

Norman said, "No fair. How come they get to play with theirs and we don't?"

"Yeah," agreed Bob. "How come? I don't get to play with mine either."

Mom said, "I wish on this tape they had said, 'Kids, don't try this at home.' "

Other scenes on the tape showed the astronauts working on different kinds of experiments. One odd thing was that a couple of them were hanging upside down.

Norman said, "They look sort of like big bats."

Bob suggested, "Maybe they're vampire astronauts."

Norman said, "I can do that hanging by my knees on the monkey bars at the playground. But you don't want to do it for very long. It makes your head feel funny, and you can fall off."

"Yeah," said Bob. "And everything falls out of your pockets. I lost two quarters that way."

Dad explained, "In space they can't tell up from

down. So there is no upside down or right side up."

Norman looked puzzled. "What about sideways?" he asked. "Is there sideways in space?"

"You got me," replied Dad. "I don't know the answer to that one."

Michael said, "Look, that's interesting."

"What?" asked Bob. "Is their money falling out?"

Michael replied, "They're not wearing shoes. All of them are wearing just socks."

Chapter 7

The countdown sign in the school lobby soon said 28, then 27, 26, 25. The halls were filling up with posted space facts. The kindergartners were not ready to write facts yet, so they drew pictures. Going down the hall seemed like walking through a book. And you had to watch where you were going or you would bump into others who kept stopping to read the walls.

From the gym came the whine and whirr of power tools. The mock-up shuttle compartments were taking shape.

They took up so much space next to the stage at the end of the vast room that, as Michael had predicted, the laps in gym class were shorter. On days when the gym teacher had them running an obstacle course, there were fewer tires, bars, and plastic cones to get through, around, and over.

Soon the building project, tools, and parent volunteers were taking up so much space that the gym teacher brought in a tape player and made all the kids do line dancing. As Michael's class clomped, stomped, shuffled, and two-stepped, Mr. Jones stuck his head out of the window of the upper deck. He yelled, "Would you quit stomping so hard? You're shaking my space shuttle!"

In the real orbiter the middeck underneath the flight deck was reached by going through two holes in the floor. This worked well if you were floating in microgravity, but not with regular gravity and no stairs.

So Mr. Jones decided to put in only one hole, a ladder, and a railing. This way, he told Mr. Leedy, "They can't fall through the hole and kill themselves."

On T minus 23 it was Michael's turn to take the class attendance sheet to the office. As he put the paper up on the counter, the school secretary answered the phone. "Oh, yes, he's been expecting your call," she said excitedly. "Just a moment, please." She hurried into Mr. Leedy's office. Michael heard her say quietly, "NASA's on the phone!"

Michael lingered, hoping to hear Mr. Leedy's side of the conversation. But the secretary came out and closed the door.

"Was there something else?" she asked.

Michael's ears felt hot with embarrassment. He shook his head and left.

By the time he got back to his room and sat down, Mr. Leedy was making an announcement. "Please pardon the interruption," he said from the PA on the wall. "This is Mission Control speaking. I have great news. NASA has arranged for us to talk to our own astronaut during the shuttle flight. We're going to have a teleconference from space!"

Kids cheered and clapped and whistled and stamped their feet.

To get ready for the teleconference, Mr. Leedy announced that the students must turn in questions by a certain day. There would be time to ask only eighteen, so they had to be selected and sent to NASA well in advance. That way Mark Fortunato could be well prepared to answer them.

Every student was encouraged but not required to turn in questions.

Bob's was, "Do things fall out of your pockets when you're upside down?"

Norman wrote: "Is there sideways in space?" and "Are astronauts neat or messy?"

Michael and Chad figured out their questions together: "If you tried to play basketball in space, could you make a basket? And could you dribble the ball?"

After Mr. Leedy sorted out all the questions, he found that out of two hundred and seventy-two turned in, one hundred and three wanted to know how astronauts go to the bathroom.

So he announced on the PA: "I want to congratulate all of you who turned in questions. I'm impressed with your scientific curiosity and the thought you've put into your questions. Many of you want to know how astronauts go to the bathroom. That's a very good question. When we get our once-in-a-lifetime chance to speak to someone up in space, however, I think that asking him how they go to the bathroom would not exactly be the best use of our opportunity. So for those of you who asked—and I'm sure we're all a little curious about how they do that—we'll post the facts in the hall. Then you'll all be well informed on that topic."

Plans for experiments to go on the mock flight moved along. Materials for growing crystals were all set. Several kinds of seeds were ready to be sprouted under different conditions. Also going along for the "ride" were two gerbils (to keep each other company), an ant farm, and a bowl of guppies. No one had figured out yet what experiments to do with the animals, bugs, or fish. On a real space flight, they would act different in microgravity. But on the ground, students would just have to watch them act regular. Since astronauts sometimes do health experiments on each other, kids practiced counting pulses, holding their necks or wrists.

Everybody in school started talking space lingo. The gym was now the VAB, for Vehicle Assembly Building. Recess was an EVA, short for extra-vehicular activity. But the first-graders just called it a "space walk." On cold days they bundled up, giggling, in their coats and mufflers, pretending they were putting on space suits. Then they space walked stiff-legged down the hall to the school's back door.

Mr. Leedy began every day's morning announcements on the PA with "T minus" however many days were left "to launch."

Countdowns could be heard all over the building for all occasions. The most popular one was: "Five, four, three, two, one, LUNCH!"

Mr. Leedy asked Michael if he had asked his parents about bringing their plants to school for the mock flight.

"I forgot," replied Michael.

"Please do it today, and let me know tomorrow," urged the principal.

Chapter 8

When the boys got home from school, Mom was on the phone with Dr. Sparks, getting a progress report on her plants' training.

After Mom hung up, she said, "Susan loves calling them plantronauts. Now the people she's working with at NASA are calling them that, too."

"Yay!" exclaimed Norman.

Michael felt annoyed that Norman's idea had gotten so popular. "How's the training going?" he asked.

"Pretty well," said Mom. "Some of her plants aren't cooperating, but Susan feels sure she'll have them all under control in time for the flight. It's amazing what she's been able to teach those plants."

"That's not so great," said Michael. "What we

taught Stanley and Fluffy is better—and what they've learned on their own is even more amazing. Stanley could learn to pick up trash and put it in a bin if he wanted to. That would be easy for him."

"Fortunately," said Mom, "ever since you promised to keep your side of your room clean in return for getting to keep Stanley, we don't need a plant to do that."

At dinner that evening, Michael ate messily as usual. Peas rolled off his fork, pattering on the floor. When he plunked his milk glass down after a hearty gulp, drips ran down onto the place mat. He stirred all the food on his plate together—mashed potatoes, meat, and the remaining peas.

"Quit rearranging it," said Mom, "and just eat it."

Norman ate his peas first, carefully stabbing each one with his fork so they couldn't roll away. Then he turned his attention to his mashed potatoes. With his spoon, he molded them into a hill in the middle and a short wall encircling it.

"What are you doing?" asked Mom.

"I'm making a castle. See? The gravy is going to go here in the moat."

"Mashed potatoes are for eating, not building," said Mom. "Quit playing with your food."

Norman replied, "The astronauts play with

their food. We're going to be pretend astronauts at school. So we should get to play with our food. Please pass the gravy."

Dad laughed. "I was just picturing what this meal would be like if we were in space," he said. "Michael, all the debris you scatter would be floating around the room—bread crumbs, peas, milk drops."

Michael replied with a grin, "We'd be floating, too. We wouldn't need chairs. We could even eat upside down." He chuckled at the thought of them all hovering in the air around a flying table.

Norman scrunched up his nose. "I wouldn't want your foodstuff bumping into my face," he said.

"One good thing," said Michael, "is it'd make you keep your mouth shut."

Mom snapped, "Stop that!" She added, "I'm glad we live on Earth where messes stay put. I wouldn't want to have to chase them around to clean them up."

Michael got a mental picture of Mom swooping through the air with the vacuum cleaner, hot on the trail of crumbs and peas that kept escaping her. He burst out laughing, and his mouthful of milk sprayed on the table and his shirt. Some came out his nose. Mom handed him a bunch of paper napkins to soak up the splatters.

She scolded, "You could choke if you're not

careful! Laugh first, then drink, not the other way around."

"I didn't know I was going to laugh," he said.

Norman bragged, "I'm always careful."

Michael dropped a dripping milk-soaked paper napkin on Norman's place mat.

"He did that on purpose!" squawked Norman.

"Time out," said Dad. "Michael, clean that up. Let's get back to having a peaceful family dinner. How did school go today?"

"Good," said Norman. "We're practicing countdowns. Want to hear me count backwards from a hundred to zero real fast?"

"Later," said Dad. Norman looked disappointed. "Right after dinner," said Dad. Norman perked up. Dad continued, "Michael, what did you do in school today?"

"We got our space facts put up in the hall. All my plants-in-space facts got picked."

"That's great," said Mom.

"Excellent," said Dad.

Michael added, "And Mr. Leedy wants to know if we can bring our plants to school for our space flight because they're related to the ones going on the real flight."

"No," said Mom and Dad together.

"Why not?" asked Norman.

Dad reminded him, "Remember the other two times the plants went to school? For the science fair and Pet Plant Day? We don't want to go through anything like that again."

Norman said, "But they mostly just act up at night! We could just take them for the day. They hardly ever do anything weird during the day. I really want Fluffy to be a plantronaut at school! Please, please, please?"

To keep Norman from arguing further, Dad said, "We'll see."

Michael asked, "What should I tell Mr. Leedy? He asked me twice."

"Tell him we're thinking it over," said Mom. "And later we'll tell him no."

"No fair," grumped Norman. "How come Dr. Sparks's plants get to be plantronauts and ours don't?"

After dinner Norman was eager to do his countdown. As soon as Dad had settled on the couch to watch the TV news, Norman asked, "Are you ready?"

"As ready as I'll ever be," replied his father.

"One hundred," began Norman. "Ninety-nine, ninety-eight, ninety-seven, ninety-six, ninety-five." Michael went back to their room to get a book about the space shuttle he was reading. From down the hall he could hear Norman droning on and on.

"Seventy-five, seventy-four, seventy-three, seventy-two, seventy-three, seventy-four—no, wait, I got mixed up. I have to start over. One hundred, ninety-nine . . ."

Dad said, "You already did that part really well. Just start where you left off."

"Where did I leave off?"

"I can't remember," said Dad. "Start at fifty."

Just then one of the TV anchors said, "The next space shuttle flight is going to have some very unusual crew members. NASA says that they're taking along some good-sized plants that may be able to perform tasks. That should be interesting. So going along with the astronauts will be plantronauts." He laughed.

His partner said, "That will be better than the fishonauts and frogonauts, which they've taken along in the past." They both laughed merrily. "Join us later tonight at eleven."

Norman yelled, "They said plantronauts! That was my idea!"

"Yes," said Dad. "It's really caught on."

Norman forgot to finish his countdown.

Chapter 9

Early the next morning Michael awoke to the sound of Norman saying, "Pick up, Fluffy. Pick up." Squinting sleepily, he saw Norman guiding one of his plant's vines to a wadded-up paper on the floor. Fluffy was poking at it but not picking it up.

"What are you doing?" asked Michael.

"I'm teaching Fluffy to pick up trash and put it in the wastebasket."

"Why? He's not going up in space."

Norman replied, "Maybe he and Stanley could do it on the school flight if we can talk Mom and Dad into letting us take them. I bet Fluffy can do it better than Dr. Sparks's plants. Fluffy's smarter than hers are. And Stanley is, too."

Michael reminded him, "Ours don't do much during the day. If we did take them to school,

49

they'd just stand around doing nothing." Fluffy pushed the paper around the floor.

"Pick up, pick up," urged Norman. Fluffy kept pushing.

Michael suggested, "Try 'grab.' That works with Stanley."

"Grab, grab," said Norman. Stanley reached over and grabbed up the crumpled paper ball. Then he tossed it toward Michael, who caught it and threw it back. His plant snatched it out of the air, and threw it again.

Michael patted Stanley's leaves. "We're not playing catch right now," he said.

"Grabbing stuff out of the air like that would work great in space," said Norman. "Fluffy and Stanley would be really good plantronauts. Better than Dr. Sparks's. If we teach ours to pick up trash, then the next time we see her, we can show off that ours are smarter." He put the paper back on the floor and began again. "Grab, Fluffy, grab."

After he had chanted this about twenty times, Fluffy finally picked up the paper. He paused for a moment as if wondering what to do with it. Then he carefully placed it on top of Norman's head.

Michael laughed. "That's a start," he said. "But this is going to take more practice."

* * *

Over the next few days, Norman gathered a bunch of trash objects for the plants' early morning practice—empty cans and plastic bottles, crumpled papers, an empty cereal box. He kept these in a plastic bag in the boys' closet. Every morning Norman awoke early and pestered Michael until he got up so they could train the plants before Mom and Dad awoke.

Michael always complained about having to get up early. But since he loved to teach Stanley and play with him, he didn't really mind being dragged out of bed for the lessons. Of course, he wouldn't admit that to Norman.

Both plants were quick learners. It wasn't long before they were getting pretty good at picking up trash and putting it into a wastebasket.

One day Mom announced, "Our committee has decided to do trial runs of space food with our own families. We want to try out these things before serving them to the whole school. That way, if there are any problems, we can make changes before the big day."

Norman asked, "Is the food going to be yucky?"

Mom replied, "I think you'll be pleasantly surprised."

Michael asked, "Can we order pizza for backup in case it turns out to be a disaster?"

"It's not going to be a disaster. There're just a few things we're not sure are going to work out."

Dad said, "That might be one of the nights I have to work late, so I'll just get something quick to eat at the office."

"We're doing it Saturday," Mom told him. "For lunch. So nobody has an excuse not to be here."

Norman asked, "Can Bob come?"

"Sure. Michael, you invite somebody, too. We'll have plenty of food. The more, the merrier."

On Saturday Bob came over well before lunchtime. He and Norman kicked a soccer ball up and down the hall for a while until Mom told them to cut it out.

She said, "I have to run over to the Kramers' for a few minutes to borrow some things I need for our space lunch. I'll be right back. Behave yourselves."

Norman asked Bob, "What do you want to do now?"

"I don't know," replied Bob. "Let's play space adventure."

"Okay," said Norman. "I've got a space helmet in the closet. I'll go get it."

He returned with the helmet and his empty Water Blaster. "This looks like a space gun," he explained.

"Let's take turns wearing the helmet," said Bob. "Me first!"

Norman really wanted to wear it himself, but

he handed it over. He ran into the living room and hopped on the couch.

"This can be our spaceship," he said. "Get in." Bob jumped on and they counted down, "Ten, nine, eight, seven, six, we have ignition!" Bob made what he thought might be ignition noises. Norman kept counting: "Five, four, three, two, one, launch!" Off they flew in their imaginations.

"We should meet some aliens," said Bob.

"Good ones or evil ones?" asked Norman.

"Evil!" declared Bob.

"Okay, look out! Here come the alien warriors! They all got Blasters filled with slime! Orange slime!" He aimed his Blaster and went "Pow! Pow! Oh, no!"

"What?" asked Bob, looking worried.

"They slimed up our windows! They're all orange! We can't see out! We're going to crash! Hold on!"

Making crash noises, they leaped off the couch and rolled on the floor, knocking aside the coffee table.

"We made it!" exclaimed Bob. "We're okay!"

"Oh, no!" shouted Norman. "Here they come again! The Alien Warriors of the Orange Slime!"

"Let's slime them back!" yelled Bob. They scrambled over the back of the couch and hid behind it. Slowly, carefully, they peeked over it. Norman aimed his Blaster. Bob aimed his finger.

"Wait till they get really close," said Norman. "Then we'll slime them right in the nose!"

Bob thought a moment. He asked, "What color's our slime?"

"Purple," decided Norman. "Purple's better than orange. We're the Earth Warriors of the Purple Slime!"

Bob suggested, "They could change to good aliens. Then we could make friends with them and they could show us their planet and give us snacks."

"Okay," said Norman, "but first let's slime them. Pow! Pow!"

Bob said, "Slime should sound more like goosh-goosh, not pow-pow."

As they shouted "Goosh, goosh," Michael wandered in, eating a banana.

He said, "Tell Mom I went over to Chad's and we'll be back in time for lunch." He added, "You two are really weird."

Bob frowned and said huffily, "We're Earth Warriors of the Purple Slime."

Michael, with his mouth full of banana, mumbled, "More like escapees from the Planet Goofball." He went out the front door.

"Don't pay any attention to him," said Norman. "Too bad we don't have any real slime. We could really get him. Let's go out in the kitchen and get some alien snacks."

54

Norman found some celery in the refrigerator, so he and Bob decided to make ants-on-a-log. They smeared two stalks with peanut butter.

"Where's the ants?" asked Bob.

Norman got a box of raisins from a cupboard. They stuck some on the peanut butter.

When Norman went to the refrigerator to get grape juice, Bob said, "One of your raisins is moving!"

"Where did that come from?" exclaimed Norman. He took his celery to the back door, plucked the real bug off, and put it outside.

"I thought we got them all," he said. "But every once in a while, there's another one." He scooped out the spot in the peanut butter where the bug had been and threw it away.

After touching the bug, Norman went to the sink to wash his hands. He pumped out a little glob of white liquid soap from the plastic bottle there and rubbed it between his fingers.

Mom always bought the liquid kind because bar soap left a mess sticking to the sinks or soap dishes that had to be cleaned up.

"Hey, this is real slimy," said Norman. He pumped some more and smeared it on Bob's hand. "See, it's slippery."

"Yeah," agreed Bob. "Too bad it's not purple." They washed their hands and went back to their snacks.

Norman got a great idea while he was sipping his grape juice. "This could make it purple," he said. He pumped a puddle of soap into a cereal dish and poured on some grape juice. He stirred it with a finger. The soap turned slightly purple but not very.

"More juice," advised Bob. That made the soap more purple but very runny.

Norman said, "It still feels slimy."

Bob suggested, "We could put some in your Blaster and take turns being the Earth Warriors and the aliens."

"Okay," said Norman, "but we better take it outside. I don't want to make a mess." From a storage cupboard he took the giant refill bottle of liquid soap. Mom always bought giant refills because soap got used up fast by the whole family, especially in the shower. Bob carried the grape juice bottle.

On the backyard grass Norman poured a little soap into the Blaster, being careful not to spill any. Bob poured in some juice. Norman shook the Blaster up, down, and sideways to mix them. But the soap coated the inside of the water gun.

"It won't blast with the soap stuck to the insides," said Norman.

"More juice," said Bob. He sloshed in a lot. This rinsed the soap into a purple runny mixture. Norman squirted a little on his hand.

"It's not slimy enough now," he said. "Too much juice. Needs more soap." That made the purple too pale. On they went, with more juice, more soap, too much, too little, until almost all the soap from the giant refill bottle was in the Blaster, and so was all the juice. Now the mix was a nice light shade of purple and slimy enough to suit Norman.

Bob asked, "Isn't your Mom going to be mad that we took all the soap?"

"No, I can squirt it back in the bottle."

Bob wondered, "Won't she notice it turned purple?"

"Some soap is pink," said Norman. "We had pink refills before." He aimed the Blaster at Bob. "Look out, alien! I, Earth Warrior of the Purple Slime, have come to capture your planet and your snacks!"

He squirted. Laughing, Bob ducked out of the way. The goo hit the grass.

"No fair," said Bob. "I should have slime, too. Orange slime! We can make some with orange juice."

"We don't have any soap left," said Norman.

Bob insisted, "Then we have to take turns. I want to be Earth Warrior, too."

Norman did not want to take turns. It was his Blaster. But Bob was his best friend. So after a lot more squirts, some of which got Bob but most of which hit the grass, Norman let him use the Blaster.

Taking turns, dodging and running, laughing and shouting, they tried to get each other with the purple slime. Both got quite a few gooey splotches on their faces, hands, jeans, and shirts. They slipped and skidded around on the slimy spots on the grass. It was hard to hold on to the Blaster with their slimed-up hands.

"It's a good thing soap washes off," said Bob.

They heard the kitchen window open. Mom yelled, "I'm back!" From where she was standing, she could hear them but not see them. "Quit horsing around and come in and wash your hands. The great space lunch will be ready in a few minutes!"

Norman said, "We better sneak in the front door." They made it to the bathroom without anyone else seeing them.

Chapter 10

Norman got washcloths for them both and turned on the faucet. Because they had so much soap on them, it really sudsed up when they applied water. Hard scrubbing, rinsing, and wiping got their faces and hands clean. But the more water they put on the soap-soaked splotches on their clothes, the sudsier they got.

"This isn't working," said Bob.

They took off their shirts and tried to rinse the soap out under the faucet, but the shirts got completely soaked.

Through the bathroom door, they heard Mom calling from the kitchen, "Norman! Bob! Come on! Lunch is ready!"

Norman stuck his head out and yelled back, "In a minute!"

"Now what?" asked Bob. Norman wrapped

their wet shirts in a towel. He peeked out to make sure the coast was clear. Then they dashed across the hall to the boys' room. Norman shoved the towel, empty soap and juice bottles, and Blaster under his bed. He got two shirts from his bureau. They wriggled into them and ran for the kitchen.

Michael, Chad, and Dad were already at the table. Norman and Bob sat down.

There were no plates—just a small pile of plastic tight-seal bags at each place.

Michael asked, "Do we have a backup pizza?"

"No," replied Mom. "First, everybody take the plastic bag on top of your pile. The one with the pink grainy stuff."

"What is this?" asked Norman.

Mom poured steaming hot water into a measuring cup. "Now open the seal on your bag halfway and watch your fingers when I pour." She went around, putting a measured amount of hot water into each bag.

"Seal it up again and shake it well to mix," she instructed. Everybody shook.

"Oh!" said Bob. "It's soup!"

Norman said, "We need bowls to put it in."

"No bowls," said Mom. "In space your soup could splash all over and hang around in the air." She passed out plastic straws. "Open a corner of your bag, just enough to put your straw in."

"Eat soup with a straw?" said Bob. "We don't do that at my house."

"We don't do it here either," said Mom. "Today this is space pretend."

Mom passed out a paper clip to everyone. "This is a clip for your straw, not exactly like astronauts use, but sort of." She showed how to put one on the middle of the straw. "This shuts off the flow between sips," she explained. "In space, any liquid in the straw when you stop drinking wouldn't fall back down. It could escape and float around when you take your mouth off the straw. Closing it with the clip keeps it from getting away."

Chad said, "That's really interesting."

"Milk is next," said Mom. "That's your bag with the white powder. For this we use cold water." They measured and poured to liquify their milk.

Michael said, "But the water could get away when you pour."

"Astronauts don't pour," said Mom. "They use a machine that sticks a needle through the plastic package and injects the water. Like getting a shot from the doctor."

"Vaccinating food with water!" exclaimed Chad. "That's amazing. Are we going to have needles to do that on space food day at school?"

"No," said Mom. "Fortunately not."

*   *   *

Meanwhile, Fluffy must have been feeling thirsty because when he found the Blaster under Norman's bed, he dragged it out. Norman had often used it to water his plant. Fluffy had even watered himself with it a few times, although his aim was not good.

In the kitchen they moved on to the next bags, which turned out to be instant mashed potatoes.

"Are we supposed to eat this through a straw?" asked Dad.

"No, squeeze it out of a corner of the bag right into your mouth." Trying to do this caused a lot of laughing.

Dad said, "You're going to have some mashed potato messes when hundreds of kids try to do this at school."

"That's why we're having a trial run," said Mom. "Some parents on our committee who have younger kids will find out today how this works with them."

Michael asked, "Do you have any powdered pizza?" Everybody laughed.

"That would be good," said Chad.

The last bag contained a peanut butter sandwich, carrot sticks, and some raisins.

"Good," said Michael. "Something that doesn't need vaccinating."

Mom said, "Just be careful not to take more

than one thing out of the bag at a time. And don't let go of it."

Dad asked, "How come the sandwich and carrots are fresh when everything else is dehydrated?"

"There's no refrigerator on the shuttle," she explained, "but they take some fresh food and eat it before it gets a chance to spoil. Remember the guy with the banana on the videotape? They do have an oven to heat prepackaged foods. They can even have steak if they want it. Or shrimp cocktail. I read in a book that one astronaut's sauce from her shrimp cocktail got loose. That must have been a sight!"

Norman asked, "Are we going to have some space dessert?"

"Yes. Chocolate pudding in pull-top cans and cookies."

"Powdered cookies?" asked Norman.

"No, regular ones. Astronauts eat regular pudding and cookies in space. Of course, the cookies are vacuum-wrapped in plastic."

Michael chuckled. "It would be funny if chocolate pudding got loose," he said. "What a great mess that would be!"

While they ate dessert, Mom passed around a small transparent plastic box half full of yellow rocks. When the boys shook the box, the rocks rattled.

"We got this from NASA," she said. "Anybody guess what it is?" Nobody knew.

"When you add hot water," she revealed, "presto! It's scrambled eggs."

Norman and Bob made gross-out noises.

Dad asked, "We don't have to eat these, do we?"

"No," said Mom. "They're just for showing at school."

Michael shook the box at Chad, making the eggs rattle.

"Scrambled rocks!" he said, laughing.

"What's that other noise?" asked Dad. They all stopped talking to listen. "It's skateboard wheels in the hall," he said. "And they're coming this way!"

Chapter 11

Fluffy zoomed into the kitchen and rolled to a stop when he bumped into Dad's chair.

"What's going on?" asked Mom. "The plants don't usually run around during the day."

Norman dashed over to Fluffy. "What's wrong?" he asked.

Fluffy lifted a vine from which a little purple slime oozed. He pointed it at the dirt in his pot. There was a lot more slime there.

"Uh, oh," said Norman.

"What's wrong?" said Mom. She took a closer look. "What is this stuff?" she asked. "And where did it come from?"

As if in answer to her question, Fluffy lifted the Blaster, which he had been dragging along behind him. Waving it around, he blasted little spurts of slime—on the wall, the floor, the ceiling, the table, Michael's cookies, Norman's hair, Mom's shoes. Bob and Chad, who had not known how the plants could act up, dove under the table.

Norman calmed Fluffy down. Michael disentangled the Blaster from the plant's clutches.

Mom sat down and took off her sneakers. The laces were gooey. "Another day," she said with a sigh, "another plant disaster!"

"It wasn't Fluffy's fault," protested Norman.

"Who put this stuff in your Blaster?"

"Uh—I did. But we were only playing with it outside so it wouldn't make a mess in the house."

"And what is this goo?"

"Uh—soap. When you put water on your shoelaces, they're going to get really, really clean. You'll see."

"Where did you get it?"

"From the refill bottle. I was going to squirt it back in the bottle. But you yelled at us to come to lunch. So I didn't have time. I was going to do it after lunch. As soon as I got a chance."

Bob said helpfully from under the table, "That's right. He was going to put it back in the bottle. He really was. He said so. Really."

Mom told Bob and Chad, "You can come out now. Just watch where you step."

She told Dad and Norman, "You guys be the Fluffy cleaning team. Take him to the bathroom for soap removal. Michael and I will wipe up this mess in the kitchen."

Bob volunteered, "I want to be on the Fluffy team, too."

"Fine," said Mom. She looked at him closely. "Norman has a shirt just like that," she said. The Fluffy team headed for the bathroom. Chad headed for the door. He called, "Bye and thanks for lunch!"

After the purple slime was all cleaned up, Norman took Fluffy back to the boys' room. Bob's mother called to tell him to come home. Norman pumped the leftover soap from the Blaster back into the refill bottle and put the soapy shirts in the laundry basket. He sat down to talk to Fluffy.

Mom and Dad went out to walk around the yard. They slipped on some purple slime in a few places on the grass.

"Wouldn't it be nice," said Mom, "if we could send the plants on a long vacation?"

"Dream on," said Dad.

In the kitchen, Michael found a couple of unslimed cookies and poured himself a glass of milk. He was the only one there when the phone rang.

It was Dr. Sparks. "I've got a big problem," she said, "and I'm calling to ask a big favor. Can I borrow your plants for the shuttle flight?"

Chapter 12

Michael was so surprised that he almost dropped the phone. He didn't know what to say.

"Are you there?" asked Dr. Sparks.

"Yes. Did something happen to your plants?"

"They refuse to cooperate. They got less and less interested in picking things up. Now they won't do it at all. They're acting like a bunch of stubborn little children who won't do what they're supposed to. Our experiment's cancelled unless I can supply another plant that can eat dirty socks and pick up trash and doesn't weigh more than my smaller ones put together. I've gotten approval for a substitute. I'm sure your plant is within the right weight—without its skateboard, of course. It won't need a skateboard in space. And your plants are good at grabbing things."

"Yes, but . . ."

"So your plant will go on the flight because the plan calls for eating dirty socks. Norman's will be the control experiment on the ground."

"But . . ." said Michael.

"Don't worry," Dr. Sparks assured him. "I'll take excellent care of them. And so will the mission specialists."

"But . . ." Michael tried again.

Dr. Sparks continued, "I need to talk this over with your parents, of course. Could you put them on the phone and tell Norman? I can't thank you enough for lending your plants. We couldn't pass up a scientific opportunity like this!"

Michael yelled for his parents. Mom took the kitchen phone. Dad picked up the one in their bedroom. Michael explained the situation to Norman.

"How come they want Stanley to go up in space and not Fluffy?" said Norman.

Michael explained that they needed one that eats dirty socks, not clean ones.

"Don't worry," he added. "Dad and Mom won't want our plants to get mixed up in anything like this. They don't even want us to take them to school for one day."

But on the phone, Mom was telling Dr. Sparks, "One of our plants flying with the astronauts!

This is thrilling! Our boys' plants will go down in scientific history. Or up in history. Or whatever."

Dad asked, "Would this cost us anything?"

"No," replied Dr. Sparks. "My research budget covers everything."

"They'd be well taken care of, wouldn't they?" asked Dad.

"Definitely," said Dr. Sparks. "Either I or one of my student assistants or a mission specialist going on the flight will be in charge of them at all times. And even while Michael's plant is in space, we'll be monitoring and communicating with the mission specialists who'll be working with the plant."

Dad said, "Then I don't see any reason not to do this—as long as it's okay with the boys."

Mom said, "I don't either." She called, "Michael? Norman? This is all right with you, isn't it?"

"I don't know," Michael answered. He didn't really want to say yes. The thought of Stanley in space was too mind-boggling. He wanted a couple of weeks to think it over. But he couldn't think of any reasons to say no fast enough.

Norman protested, "Fluffy wouldn't like going away without me. He'd be lonesome." Michael knew that unless Norman had recently learned how to do plant mind-reading he was really talking about his own feelings.

Mom noticed that Norman looked glum.

She said, "Fluffy will be doing important scientific work. And Susan will take good care of him."

"Okay," Norman agreed.

"Michael?" asked Mom. "Okay?"

"I guess so. Yeah."

She told Dr. Sparks, "The boys said okay."

"Great," said Dr. Sparks. "I'll call you back later about what time tomorrow a truck will come to pick up the plants. It's air-conditioned and heated, so they'll have a safe and comfortable trip."

Norman went to tell Fluffy. Michael found him in their room with one arm around his plant's main stalk.

"Fluffy's worried," said Norman, "even though he's going to be doing important science work."

Michael could see who was worried. It wasn't Fluffy.

"At least your plant'll stay on the ground," said Michael. "Dr. Sparks will be with him the whole time. He'll be fine." He sat down on his bed next to Stanley.

"You're going on a space adventure," he told his plant. "To boldly go where no big plant has gone before." He stroked Stanley's leaves. This whole thing really was thrilling, he thought.

Norman asked, "Will Stanley have to go on the Vomit Comet?"

"I hope not," replied Michael. That started him worrying about all the things that could go wrong.

71

Chapter 13

That afternoon the family got the plants ready for the trip. Mom helped the boys dust and polish Stanley's and Fluffy's leaves. Dad cleaned the wheels on their skateboards. Norman packed a lunch for Fluffy, a five-day supply of white socks with brown stripes around the top. These were Fluffy's favorite flavor, what Norman and Michael called fudge ripple. Michael changed his socks twice during the day as usual to get enough pairs smelled up for Stanley's nightly dinner.

That night, with all the excitement, the boys had trouble going to sleep. Lying in bed, Norman was holding one of Fluffy's vines and counting down from one hundred. He kept getting mixed up and starting over.

"Forty-seven, forty-six, forty-five," he droned

on. "Do you think," he wondered aloud, "the astronauts will feed Stanley powdered socks?"

"No," said Michael.

"I mean with water added."

"No."

Norman was silent for a few moments. Just when Michael hoped he had gone to sleep, he started up again: "Fifty-seven, fifty-six, fifty-five."

Michael complained, "You're going backwards."

"Am not."

"I mean you skipped backwards from where you left off."

"Where did I leave off?"

"Twenty-two." But Norman did not fall for that.

"That's not backward," he said. "That's forward." He began again. "Seventy-six, seventy-five, seventy-four, seventy-three, seventy-four, seventy-five." He got all the way back to eighty before he realized what he was doing.

He said, "Maybe while Fluffy's away, I can talk to him on the phone."

Michael said kiddingly, "And maybe you can write him letters."

"Plants can't read," replied Norman as if any fool should know that. "Sixty-four, sixty-three, sixty-two, sixty-three, no, wait. Sixty-two, sixty-one."

"Grrr," said Michael. He rolled over and

pressed the sides of his pillow over his ears. Trying to tune Norman out, he pictured Stanley floating in space. He looked light and graceful, like he was having fun. Michael fell asleep.

Norman droned on for a few more minutes before he fell asleep. Fluffy tucked the covers up under his chin and patted him on the head.

Late that night Stanley and Fluffy picked up their sock meals from the floor and sucked them into the ice cream cone–shaped leaves they used for eating. Their schlurps were followed in a little while by hearty burps and an "ex" from Fluffy. This would be their last regular meal at home in their familiar room for quite a while.

Sunday afternoon the truck pulled into the driveway right on time. Two men got out and introduced themselves as Dr. Sparks's assistants, Matt and Sam.

"Don't worry," said Matt. "We'll take very good care of your plants. And I'll ride in back with them all the way."

The boys helped Matt and Sam roll Fluffy and Stanley up a ramp placed behind the truck. Inside were two high wooden corrals lined with thick padding. These fenced the plants in so they could not fall over or roll around while the truck was moving. Dad checked to be sure they were safely fastened.

Matt asked Michael, "Do these plants have to have their sock meals cut up in little pieces like the ones Dr. Sparks trained?"

"No, they eat them whole. Six dirty ones a night for Stanley, five clean ones for Fluffy. But on days when they get outside for more sunlight, they don't eat so much."

Matt said, "For shuttle training they won't be outside at all."

Michael informed him, "When you want them to grab something like trash, you have to tell them 'Grab' or they won't do it. Unless it's something they want to grab anyway. Stanley likes to get towed by grabbing onto bicycles. But there aren't any bicycles on the shuttle, so you don't have to worry about that."

"The crew has exercise equipment to keep up their muscle strength. Your plant can grab onto those if it wants."

When Norman went back in the house to get Fluffy's lunch bag, Michael got up the nerve to ask Matt a question that was bothering him: "To get ready for the flight, will my plant have to go on the Vomit Comet?"

"No," said Matt. "That's just for people, to get them used to feeling weightless."

"Do you think my plant will get motion sickness in space?"

"No. Astronauts often get it, but I don't think

a plant will have that problem." He smiled and added, "Besides, plants don't vomit. At least, not any that I know of, and I've studied a lot of botany."

Norman climbed the ramp into the truck to stay with Fluffy until the last minute.

"Be good," he said. "Do your experiments just like Dr. Sparks wants. And eat your socks every night."

"We have to get going," said Sam.

Norman gave his plant a big hug. Fluffy wrapped his vines around Norman, who almost disappeared in the greenery.

Michael did not want to make such a big fuss about saying goodbye to Stanley.

"Behave yourself," he said. "Have fun with the astronauts. You'll be back before we know it." Stanley put a vine around Michael's shoulder. Michael patted the vine.

"See you," called Michael as he went down the ramp. Stanley waved.

Matt pulled the ramp in. He closed the big doors, shutting himself in with the plants. The family watched as Sam drove the truck down the street, around the corner, and out of sight. Stanley and Fluffy were gone.

Chapter 14

A half hour later, Norman started whining: "I'm bored. I miss Fluffy."

Mom suggested, "Occupy your mind with something else."

"Like what?"

"Play with Bob. Get out some of your old games that you like." Norman looked totally uninterested. "Read a book. Or how about a movie? Let's go to the library and the video store. We can make some popcorn and watch a movie."

"Oh, all right," said Norman grumpily.

The whole family went along. At the library, they all found books that they wanted to read. But at the video store they could not agree on which movie to rent. Dad wanted a western. Mom wanted a comedy. Michael wanted a space adventure. Norman didn't want any of those.

Dad finally decided, "All right, let's splurge and rent one for each of us. That way, everybody can have what they want. And if anybody wants to watch anybody else's movie, that's fine—but you don't have to."

Dad, Mom, and Michael stepped up to the checkout counter with their selections. Norman was still wandering the aisles, looking at every video.

"Come on," said Michael impatiently.

"I'm looking for a plant movie," replied Norman.

"There aren't any plant movies," said Mom. "Quit dawdling and just pick something." She told Dad, "I'll go ahead and get the things we need at the drugstore and meet you at the car."

Norman finally found a plant movie, *Little Shop of Horrors*. He handed it to Dad at the counter.

Dad said, "Isn't this the one about the flower shop that grows a monster plant that eats people and sings at the same time?"

"Yeah, it's great!"

"We already saw that one," said Dad. "Once was enough."

"But there aren't any other plant movies," complained Norman. "I need a plant movie to cheer me up."

"Keep looking," said Dad.

Finally Norman returned from the back of the store. "I got one!" he said, waving a video.

Dad glanced at it. "Oh, no. That's that awful *Swamp Monster* horror movie that your mother hates. It's the one she says gave her nightmares when she saw it when she was little."

Norman protested, "This isn't the same one. It's a sequel. See?" He pointed to the small print that said *Son of* above the big lettering of *Swamp Monster*.

"We don't want you watching horror movies."

"This isn't a horror movie. It's a monster movie!"

"The first one horrified your mother."

"It won't scare me. I know the swamp monster is a guy in a glop suit. Just special effects. But he's partly a plant. In the picture on the box on the shelf he has vines all over him. This movie'll cheer me up."

Dad gave in.

When they met Mom at the car, she was not pleased about Norman's selection. Dad said, "Maybe he's old enough now to watch something like that."

Mom told Norman, "But if it scares you silly, remember I told you so." She turned to Dad. "And if he wakes up in the middle of the night with nightmares from this, you get to get up with him."

*   *   *

When the family returned home, Dad went down the street to visit a friend. Michael went to Chad's to help him put together a spaceship model. Norman invited Bob over to watch *Son of Swamp Monster*.

Mom told them, "I'll be in my room. I'm going to call my mother. And I've got a good book I want to read. Call me when your movie's over. Then I'll watch mine."

Norman and Bob sprawled on the couch. Norman pressed the play button on the remote.

"This is going to be really scary," he said.

"Yeah," said Bob. "This is great!" The movie began with spooky music and the parts that said who was in the movie and who made it.

Bob asked, "Aren't we going to have popcorn? We always do with movies at my house."

"OK," agreed Norman. He pressed stop. Bob followed him to the kitchen. Norman rummaged around in the pots and pans cupboard and hauled out the bottom of the popcorn popper. He put in some oil and a lot of corn kernels. He plugged it in. "It takes a long time to heat up," he said.

"At my house we always make it in the microwave," said Bob.

"This is how my mom always makes it," said Norman. "She lets me make it sometimes."

"At my house, it pops in a paper bag," said Bob. "Do you put a paper bag on this for the popcorn to go in?"

"No, a plastic thing goes on top. Then the machine spits the popcorn out in the top. Rat-a-tat-tat! When it's done, you turn the whole thing over and the top is a big bowl full of popcorn." He looked for the top. But it was not in the part of the cupboard where the bottom had been. He started taking pots and pans out and stacking them on the floor so he could burrow into the cupboard to search. Soon just his legs were sticking out.

"Do you see it yet?" asked Bob.

"I know it's in here somewhere," said Norman. "Get me a flashlight out of that drawer by the sink."

Bob looked in the drawer, but the flashlight wasn't there. "I can't find it," he said. "You better come find it yourself."

Norman tried to wiggle out. "I'm sort of stuck," he said. "Pull on my feet!"

Bob grabbed Norman's sneakers by the heels and pulled. The shoes came off in his hands. "Oops," said Bob.

They heard a loud POP. A fluffy white kernel flew through the air and landed on the floor.

"Hurry up and help me out of here," said Norman. "One pop means the rest's going to go any minute."

Bob yanked on Norman's feet again. This time he budged him enough so he could back himself out. As he emerged, there was a loud POP POPPITY POP POP POP. More kernels shot up through the air.

"Did you find the top?" asked Bob.

"No, we have to find something else to cover it. Maybe a big bowl."

"A big paper bag," said Bob. "Have you got any?"

"Mom keeps those under the sink." Norman started for the sink on his hands and knees. But it was too late. POP, POP, POPPITY POPPITY, POP, POP, POP! Flying corn sailed overhead, landing all over the kitchen. While Norman tried to find a bag, Bob ran around trying to catch the popcorn in a pan. He caught quite a few pieces before they hit the floor and put them in his mouth. "This is fun!" he exclaimed. "Look! No hands!" he yelled, running around with his mouth open. He caught a few that way but kept bumping into the table and chairs.

Seeing this, Norman could not resist joining in. There was so much popcorn exploding into the air that they could not help catching some in their mouths. He figured he could sweep up the mess as soon as the popping stopped.

The poppity-popping made so much noise that they did not hear Mom call: "Norman, turn off your movie for a minute and pick up the kitchen phone! Grandma wants to say hi to you!" When he did not pick up the phone, she came looking for him.

Chapter 15

Mom flung open the kitchen door. Norman and Bob skidded to a halt. Popcorn rained down upon them all.

Mom crunched across the littered floor and unplugged the popper. But until it cooled off, it kept throwing corn.

She picked up the kitchen phone and said, "Mother? I have to call you back. Norman and his friend have just filled the kitchen with popcorn. They have also taken the pots and pans out of the cupboard and stacked them on the floor. Don't ask me why. I don't know. I'll talk to you later."

She brushed popcorn off her hair.

"Have you lost your minds?" she asked.

"No," replied Norman. "Just the top to the popper."

"You two are now the popcorn cleaning team. Get the broom and dustpan. And don't eat any of the corn on the floor."

Norman asked, "Can we eat the ones that fell on the table? The table's not dirty."

"Okay, but first clean up the rest of the kitchen. It looks like it's been snowing in here."

After the boys finished their chore, they found that Mom had taken over the VCR and was watching her movie. Bob decided to go home. Norman walked partway with him. On the way back, he saw his favorite neighbor, Mrs. Smith, out in her yard. She was clipping some overgrown bushes.

"What's new?" she asked. Her small brown dog, Margo, came running over to Norman, wagging her tail. He patted her side. Margo flopped on the grass and rolled over to have her tummy rubbed.

Norman told Mrs. Smith about Dr. Sparks using their plants for the NASA experiment.

"That's really wonderful!" she said. "I wondered what that truck was doing at your house," she said. "But I couldn't come over then because I was on the phone talking to Shawn and Belinda. I was hoping you'd come over and tell me what was going on. And if you didn't, I was going to stop by and ask."

She added, "I suppose you'll miss your plant while it's away."

Norman nodded.

"Well, if you get lonesome," she said, "come over anytime and visit my African violets. And Margo and I are always glad to see you, too."

Norman noticed something new standing by Mrs. Smith's front door. It was a gray statue of a goose about two feet high.

"Where'd you get that?" he asked.

"It's a present from Shawn and Belinda. They wanted to give me a gift for organizing their wedding and asked me what I wanted. It was delivered yesterday."

"What's it for?"

"It's a yard decoration. Some people have little statues of rabbits or frogs in their gardens, but these geese are really popular. They're made out of concrete. I thought it would be fun to have one."

"It looks nice," said Norman.

"Wait till you see it all dressed up! That's why these are so popular. People dress them up in little outfits. There are stores that sell goose costumes for every occasion. I love to sew, so I can make my own. I'm going to make a Santa suit with a little white beard for December. And a turkey suit for November. Maybe in April bunny ears and a basket. Do you think a pumpkin outfit or a witch costume would be better for Halloween?"

"A ghost suit would be good," said Norman.

"Perfect!" exclaimed Mrs. Smith. "You always have such good ideas!"

"And a football uniform," he suggested.

"Yes, of course!"

Norman said, "Maybe you can make some outfits for Margo, too."

Mrs. Smith laughed. "Margo probably wouldn't sit still for that. She's too wiggly. Hey, I just thought of something that would be great. In honor of your plants being in the space program, I'll make my goose a little space suit outfit. With a helmet."

Monday morning Mr. Leedy caught up with Michael in the hall. "What did your parents say about bringing your plants to school for our mock flight?"

"Our plants can't come," Michael replied. "NASA needs them for the real flight."

Mr. Leedy chuckled. "Very funny," he said. "Now what did your parents say?"

"No, really. Our botanist friend's plants didn't work. So she needed ours. Mine's going up in space. My brother's has to be in the experiment, too, only on the ground. We just found out Saturday. They were picked up yesterday."

Mr. Leedy exclaimed, "This is wonderful! Now we not only have an Edison School astronaut. We have Edison School plantronauts, too!" He announced it to the whole school on the PA.

All day other kids came up to Michael and Norman to tell them they were really lucky.

Chapter 16

At school plans for the teleconference were moving along. A hookup with NASA's special cable channel was arranged. Mr. Leedy rented a video projector to show the broadcast in huge size on a white wall in the cafeteria. The telephone company would set up the link to connect the student questioners to the astronauts.

The day after the teleconference, the mock flights in the gym would begin and go on for a week. Student teams were organized to take turns as astronauts, launch control, and mission control. Mrs. Black explained, "The astronauts are the ones we see on TV, but there are hundreds of other people who work on these flights."

In Michael's class, Kimberly Offenberg was chosen as mission commander for their team. Michael was a mission specialist in charge of some experiments.

Every day after school Michael and Norman raced home in time for Dr. Sparks's phone call to let them know how Stanley and Fluffy were doing.

The plants made fast progress with their training to pick up trash and put it in a metal bin that they learned to open and close.

"Training, training, training," complained Norman. "Doesn't she ever let them have fun?"

At first, she reported, Stanley did not eat his usual amount. He seemed to have trouble getting used to eating other people's dirty socks. So Dr. Sparks asked Michael to send some of his dirty ones. He put them into a tight-seal plastic bag to keep in the familiar flavor of his sweaty feet. Then every morning Mom put the bag in a padded envelope addressed to Dr. Sparks, and took it to an overnight delivery service.

Dr. Sparks and her assistants fed Stanley a nightly meal of five of Michael's socks and another dirty one from one of the astronauts going on the flight. Gradually they increased the number of astronauts' socks and fed him fewer snacks from home. Stanley got along well on this menu. Soon he was completely switched over to astronauts' socks. Dr. Sparks saved Michael's extras to send along on the flight in case of possible sock-eating crises in space.

But Fluffy was not doing so well. At first he ate little. Dr. Sparks thought he would soon become used to his new surroundings and get back to normal. But he ate less and less.

One evening when Michael answered the phone, it was Matt. "We need some advice on how to handle the one called Fluffy," he said. "It looks droopy and won't eat its socks. We've tried to coax it to eat, but nothing's working."

Michael asked, "Are you sure the socks are clean fudge ripple ones?"

"Yes, we've followed instructions exactly. Brand new fudge ripple, right out of the package."

"I'll get my brother," Michael said. "He's the Fluffy expert." He yelled for Norman and explained the problem before giving him the phone.

Norman told Matt, "I know how to make him feel better. Hold the phone up to Fluffy."

"Okay," said Matt. "I'm holding it."

"Fluffy," said Norman. "I miss you. You'll be coming home soon. It won't be too long."

Matt exclaimed, "Hey! The plant just grabbed the receiver out of my hand!"

Norman grinned. "Fluffy, you know it's me, don't you!" To cheer Fluffy up, Norman did something that his plant really liked. He started singing "Oh, Susannah," slightly off-key.

As his long-distance howling came over the phone, Matt shouted, "The plant's perking up! This is amazing!"

Norman gave the song a big ear-splitting finish.

Matt said, "The plant's hugging the phone!"

Norman said, "Fluffy, be sure to eat your socks. You know they're good for you, and you like them. Come on," he added in the tone of voice Mom had used to coax him to eat his vegetables when he was little. "Eat up. They'll make you grow big and strong. Yum, yum." There was a moment of silence. Norman heard vines rustling.

Matt whispered into the phone, "It's picking up a sock."

Then Norman heard the familiar sound that told him Fluffy was feeling better: "Schlurrrrp!" He waited for the burp and "Ex" before he hung up.

After that, in addition to the daily afternoon call from Dr. Sparks, Matt made a nightly call for Norman to talk and sing to Fluffy.

Dr. Sparks told them that since she and Matt were calling them so often, she had programmed their number into the speed dialing on the lab phone. All she or her assistants had to do was press one button.

When Mr. Jones's shuttle mock-up was ready, he proudly showed it off. It was smaller than the real one, of course, and didn't look like an orbiter on the outside. But when he led Mr. Black's class in for a tour, Michael thought the inside was great.

The part where they entered was a room representing the crew deck. A couple of sleeping bags hung on the wall. Two furniture units with many drawers stood on opposite walls.

"These are like the lockers on the walls in the real shuttle," Mr. Jones pointed out. "A place for everything, and everything in its place," he added. One drawer had a sign that said "Space Snacks."

Jason opened it. "It's a fake," he said. "There's nothing in here."

Mrs. Black said, "It's going to have goodies in it when you take off."

A short ladder led to a round hole in the ceiling, the way to the flight deck above.

The kids took turns climbing into the flight deck. It was full of switches, lights, computers, and padded seats. The microphone usually used for assemblies in the gym was hooked up by the pilots' seats. Windows like the ones in the real shuttle looked out on a photomural view of Earth from space set up on the stage.

Back down in the crew deck, a door opened into a long sort of a room made of moveable walls on wheels with a tentlike roof.

"This is supposed to be the Spacelab unit in the payload bay," Mr. Jones said. "It doesn't look too good, but we added it at the last minute after we ran out of money for the project. We'll put tables in here to put the experiments on."

"You've done a wonderful job," said Mrs. Black.

Mr. Jones replied modestly, "I had a lot of help. Parents building and painting. Donated materials." He pointed to a two-way baby monitor. "We've got those in every part," he said, "for an intercom."

Jason muttered to Michael, "We don't need those. This whole thing is so small we could just yell to each other."

Mr. Jones heard him. "An intercom will be more fun," he said, frowning.

He explained that the Ground Control crew, who would handle the launch, and Mission Control, who would take over after that, would broadcast from the PA in the school office. This could be heard in the gym. The astronauts would talk on the microphone in the flight deck so everyone in the gym could hear them. The baby monitors would also send what the astronauts said to another baby monitor in the office. But because these mock flights would be going on for a week with different crews, they could not be on the PA and gym mike all day long. So they would just use the baby monitors.

Chapter 17

The morning of the real launch, when Michael left the house on his way to school, he saw Mrs. Smith's goose decked out in a little space suit and helmet. In her window was a sign that said: "Go, Stanley!"

Using a script many students had researched and written, the ones chosen by drawing lots took turns announcing stages of the countdown on the PA. Takeoff was scheduled for 10:09 a.m.

Teachers passed out the mission patches. The art classes had silk-screened them on cloth and cut them out. The winning design was a drawing of the school building with bird wings on top and rocket engines on the bottom. Lettering around the outside said, "Edison School Space Shuttle Mission." Everyone pinned their patches to their sleeves or shirt fronts. They could sew them on at home later if they wanted to.

Although the other classes were just going to sit upright in their chairs, Mrs. Black's class had decided to sit more like the astronauts. Since the shuttle was pointed up for takeoff, the crew would be lying down in their seats. So the class tipped their chairs over, with backs on the floor. They lay down in them, with their heads on the floor and knees up, bent over the front legs.

"T minus four minutes," said the PA.

"This is uncomfortable," said Pat Jenkins.

Mrs. Black said, "The astronauts have padded seats. So let's pretend we do, too. It's just for a few minutes."

Michael hoped that Stanley also had a padded seat.

Jason said, "This is boring. Aren't we going to do anything besides just lay here?"

Kimberly Offenberg said, "Launch control and the computers are running things. We don't do anything until we get to space."

Pat said, "Not doing anything with our feet in the air is really boring."

Mrs. Black said, "I'm sure the real astronauts are not bored."

Chad said, "They're probably very nervous. I feel nervous just thinking about taking off, and we're not even really going anywhere."

"I'm not bored," said Brad Chan.

"Me neither," added Michael.

Mrs. Black laughed. "When I was studying to make my dream of becoming a teacher come true," she said, "I never dreamed that some day my class and I would be lying on the floor in our chairs pretending to take off for space. When you're a teacher, you're always learning new things!"

"T minus three," said the PA.

Mrs. Black suggested, "For the next few moments let's put ourselves in the astronauts' places. If you were a real astronaut waiting to go up, what would you be thinking about right now? Since we're all lying down, I can't see you raise your hands very well. When you have something to say, raise your foot."

Several feet popped up, eagerly waving for the teacher's attention. Since Mrs. Black also could not see their faces from where she was, she called on them by their shoes: "The black sneakers with the lime-green neon laces." "The blue sneakers with the pink socks." "The brown lace-up boots."

The answers were varied:

"What if we get stuck in space and can't get back ever?"

"I'm worried that my sister might forget to feed my gerbils. Or maybe while I'm gone my gerbils will get to like her better than me."

"I'm scared about the taking-off part, but I think we'll be all right when we get there."

"I want to see what Earth looks like from space."

"I hope our experiments work right."

"I can hardly wait to get back home, and we haven't even left yet."

"Are we going to do space walks? That will be exciting!"

"I hope I don't get air sick."

"Is there a phone to call home? Because if there isn't, my mom's going to worry."

"Everybody will see us on TV."

"It's going to be fun to float in the air."

The question that made everyone laugh was from Michael: "Did we pack enough pizzas?"

Mr. Jones, walking down the hall, glanced in at their open door and saw the waving feet.

"Some rooms do sock puppet shows," he muttered to himself. "This must be a shoe puppet show they're practicing. Weird, very weird."

When the countdown got to one minute, a different but familiar voice took over. Norman had drawn the lot to count the last sixty seconds! Michael was afraid he would mess up, but Norman sailed along perfectly. Apparently all his practice had worked. When Norman got to ten, Michael was sure he couldn't mess up from there. On went Norman: "Nine. Eight. Seven. Six. Five.

Four. Three. Two. One. Zero. Lunch! I mean, launch!" Norman was squealing with excitement. "I forgot ignition! We have ignition! Yeah, and lift-off! That, too!"

The next voice took over: "We're going a hundred miles an hour, making a turn, now straight up through the thickest part of the atmosphere. The engines throttle up, faster and faster. T plus one minute, forty seconds. We're one hundred thousand feet above Earth."

Another voice: "T plus two minutes. The separation rockets fire on the two white solid fuel rocket boosters. The boosters fall away. Parachutes pop out to slow their fall toward the ocean. Boats will come to find them and tow them back to Florida to be used again."

"Now our orbiter's still riding on the giant orange liquid fuel tank. Up, up, up!"

At T plus eight and a half minutes, they reached their destination, one hundred and sixty miles above Earth. The giant tank, its liquid fuel used up, had fallen away, burning up and disintegrating.

"We're in orbit," announced Mr. Leedy. "You can get out of your seats now. Welcome to space, everyone. Our space lunch will be served in the cafeteria at T plus twenty-seven minutes."

Everyone got off the floor and picked up their chairs. Chad and Michael moved very slowly, as if they were really in space. Everybody else copied them, even Mrs. Black. They were all laughing.

Mr. Jones passed by their door and glanced in again.

"Weirder and weirder," he mumbled to himself.

The class got out their pencils, very slowly, to figure out what time T plus twenty-seven minutes was.

"It's really amazing," commented Mrs. Black, "that it only takes eight and a half minutes to get a hundred and sixty miles up in space."

Kim said, "It felt like a lot longer."

"Yes, it did," agreed Mrs. Black. "Just for fun, let's figure out how long it would take if we went a hundred and sixty miles in a car at sixty miles an hour."

Then they figured out how long it would take by plane, train, bicycle, sailboat, skateboard, and covered wagon. By the time they came up with the answers, it was almost time to eat.

They counted down together as they moved in spacey slow motion to line up at the door: "Five, four, three, two, one, zero, lunch!" Then they launched themselves much more speedily down the hall toward the cafeteria.

The space lunch was a big hit. Lots of parent volunteers had come in to help and try to prevent major plastic bag spills while kids mixed their milk and fruit drinks. Mr. Jones stood by with mop and pail, ready for flood control, but there were few messes to clean up, mostly just mashed potato mishaps.

Michael and Chad started eating in slow motion, but that took too long and they were too hungry. They went back to regular Earth speed.

As school was letting out, Mr. Leedy told Michael, "The cable channel will be connected late this afternoon. And Mr. Jones will hook up the video projector. We'll be trying out the system when the shuttle crew's scheduled to broadcast early this evening. Would you and your family like to come and watch then? I know you must be concerned about your plant. Maybe you can get a glimpse of it."

"That'd be great!" said Michael. "What time should we come?"

"About seven."

"Okay. See you then," said Michael. "Thanks, Mr. Leedy!"

Chapter 18

Mom had a big pile of paperwork she had to finish for her part-time job, so she couldn't go. "I promised to get this done tonight," she explained, "so I can take the morning off to go to the tele-conference. You guys go ahead without me."

Dad drove the boys to school after dinner, and Mr. Leedy unlocked the front door to let them in.

In the cafeteria Mr. Jones was setting up the video projector. All the tables had been folded and stacked to make room for the crowd expected for the teleconference.

Mr. Leedy told Mr. Jones, "Call me when you get it working. I'll be in my office. I've got some work to do."

Michael and Norman sat down on the floor to wait. Dad took a close look at the projector.

Mr. Jones explained, "This makes the television picture huge, like a movie." He fiddled with the controls.

Dad remarked, "It would be great to have one of these at home for watching sports."

"It sure would," replied Mr. Jones.

"And for cartoons!" added Norman.

"What's your favorite?" asked Mr. Jones as he tried several switches, trying to get a picture.

" 'Darkwing Duck,' " said Norman. "It's got my favorite evil villain, Dr. Bushroot. He's a duck scientist that accidentally turned himself into a plant. Except he still looks a lot like a duck."

"I can't quite picture that," said Mr. Jones.

"You should watch it," advised Norman. "Dr. Bushroot gets trees and bushes and flowers to help do his evil deeds. I really like plant stories, but 'Darkwing Duck' is good even when Dr. Bushroot isn't on."

Michael was staring at the white wall where the projector was aimed. An enormous rectangle appeared, full of moving fuzzy objects. As Mr. Jones worked on focusing the picture, the fuzzy objects turned into two floating astronauts, a man and a woman, whose shoulder-length hair floated around her head. They were in what looked like a narrow room with white metal drawers on the walls. Michael recognized these as lockers where astronauts keep their things to prevent them from floating all over.

"Wow!" exclaimed Dad. "Live and direct from space!"

"Amazing!" remarked Mr. Jones.

Michael asked, "Can we hear them?"

Mr. Jones said, "I think I have the sound on okay, but they're not saying anything."

Then a woman's voice from Mission Control in Houston and one of the astronauts started talking to each other about technical things.

Norman asked Michael, "Where's Stanley?"

"I don't know," said Michael. "He has to be around there somewhere."

One astronaut was talking about feeling nauseous from motion sickness. He had thrown up his first dinner in space. Michael hoped that he had thrown up into a plastic bag and not in midair.

Another talked about having trouble getting used to feeling weightless. This was his first space flight. Using too much force to move around had sent him slamming into the walls, but he was slowly getting the hang of it.

"Time to work with the plant," said another voice. Mark Fortunato pulled himself into the picture while the others moved out of the way. Michael saw a vine poke into view.

"Here comes Stanley!" yelled Norman. The whole plant moved into the picture with Mark pulling it along. The astronaut held up an empty drink bag.

"Trash grab," he commanded. "Grab." Stanley was not interested. Mark tapped the end of one of the plant's vines. Stanley curled the vine around the bag and held it, as if trying to decide what to do with it.

"Trash grab," Mark repeated. Now the plant seemed to understand what to do. With another vine, Stanley pulled on the handle of a trash locker on the floor, yanked it open, and dropped the bag in. He had a little trouble closing the locker, so Mark helped him.

"Good job, plantronaut," said Mark, grinning. "Now you get to eat dinner." He pulled off one of his socks and moved away, leaving the sock dangling in midair. Michael was glad to see it was a fudge ripple. But in moving away, Mark bumped the sock with his elbow. The sock started moving in the opposite direction. When Stanley grabbed at where it had been, it was somewhere else. The plant made several more quick grabs, causing air currents that kept the sock moving.

Michael thought Stanley looked confused. He was used to socks that stayed put. He had never had to chase his dinner around before.

Mark moved the plant out of the picture, caught the sock and held it still. A vine snatched it away. As Mark started on another experiment, the watchers in the cafeteria heard, "Schlurrrp!"

"He made it!" said Michael. Now he could relax. Stanley had done his first trash pickup all right and eaten part of his dinner. In a few moments they would hear the usual burp.

Mr. Jones had been watching all this with his mouth hanging open. "I knew your plant was very weird, from the two times you brought it to school. But not this weird," he said.

As astronauts went in and out of the picture, talking to Mission Control and doing various activities, Stanley zoomed past the camera. When he disappeared, Michael heard a klunk.

"I think he was going too fast," said Norman.

Stanley zoomed by again in the opposite direction, a little more slowly this time. He was paddling with his vines as if he were swimming.

Mr. Leedy came into the cafeteria. "I thought you were going to call me when it was working," he said.

"I got too interested watching," replied Mr. Jones. "I've never seen anything like this before!"

Stanley glided by again, waving a vine as if to say hello. But this time he was upside down.

"What on Earth was that?" exclaimed Mr. Leedy.

"It's not on Earth," said Mr. Jones. "It's that weird plant—doing aerial acrobatics."

Stanley sailed by once more. He was lying sideways and whirling like a top.

"See?" Norman told Dad. "There *is* sideways in space!"

Dad told Michael, "I think Stanley's getting overexcited."

Mr. Jones said, 'If those astronauts have any sense, they'll put a space suit on that plant and take it outside on a leash for a space walk until it calms down."

Norman started giggling about the idea of Stanley in a space suit. Then Michael realized he had not yet heard Stanley burp. Maybe his plant had been too far away from the microphone when that happened.

But no. They heard a noise that sounded like a cross between a gag and a burp.

"Look out!" yelled Mark. A mangled object flew toward him. Mark caught it and said, "Oh, yuck!"

"What is that?" asked Mr. Leedy.

Michael told him. It was a fudge ripple sock, partly digested.

Chapter 19

In the shuttle Mark was saying, "I've never heard of a plant getting motion sickness, but apparently this one just made scientific history." He asked Mission Control to ask Dr. Sparks what to do next.

Michael remembered how he had felt the time he got seasick when Dad took him fishing in a boat when he was little. So he knew that although Stanley must feel terrible, he would get better soon.

After a few minutes, Mission Control relayed advice from Dr. Sparks to make the plant stay still by zipping him into the big sleeping bag that had been made especially to fit him. Then Mark should try feeding him another sock in about an hour.

The boys and Dad waited around, watching the

astronauts go about their business, but there was no further sight or mention of Stanley. About half an hour before they were supposed to try feeding Stanley again, the shuttle broadcast ended. The NASA channel started showing a program explaining space flight.

"According to the schedule," said Mr. Leedy, "that's it from space for tonight." Mr. Jones turned off the equipment.

"But what about Stanley?" asked Michael. "We have to find out if he's okay."

Dad said, "Don't worry. When we get home, we'll wait half an hour and then call Susan. She'll be in touch with Mission Control. She'll know how he's doing. Even though the shuttle isn't televising, they still talk back and forth."

Mom had her work spread all over the dining room table. When she heard them come in the door, she said, "Susan called right after the plant emergency to let us know. I told her you were over at the school watching, and she said not to worry. She'll call back after they try to feed Stanley."

The boys told Mom all about what they had seen.

Dad asked her, "Did you get a lot of work done?"

"Yes, but I've been getting interrupted with nuisance phone calls. When I run to answer and say hello, nobody answers back. I can tell there's somebody there, but whoever it is keeps calling and saying nothing. I just hang up, but it's really irritating."

Dad said, "We can report it to the phone company and the police in the morning."

Michael asked Mom, "How do you know somebody's there if they don't say anything?"

"I heard something stirring."

"What did it sound like?" asked Dad.

"I don't know exactly. Sort of like a rustling noise."

"Rustling?" said Norman. "Like leaves?"

The phone rang.

Dad got up to answer it.

"I hope it's not the nuisance caller again," said Mom.

"It's probably Susan," said Dad.

"No," Mom said. "It's too early for her to call back."

Mom and the boys followed Dad into the kitchen. He picked up the phone.

"Hello," he said. "Hello?" He put his hand over the receiver. "No answer," he said. "It does sound like something rustling." He started to hang up.

"Wait," yelled Norman. "It might be for me!" He grabbed the phone from Dad and listened.

"Fluffy, is that you?" He kept listening. "It's him!" he exclaimed. "I know his rustling!"

From the phone came a loud "Burp!" Norman was delighted.

"Fluffy called me up to tell me he ate a good dinner," he said. The burp was followed by Fluffy's usual "Ex." Norman chatted on happily to his plant, telling him to be good and do his experiments and eat his socks. He told him all about what had happened to Stanley tonight in space.

Dad asked, "How can a plant make a long-distance phone call? Or any phone call?"

Mom explained, "Susan mentioned a while back that she programmed our number into the speed dialing on the phone in the lab where the plants were being trained because she was calling us every day. All Fluffy would have to do is pick up the receiver and press one button—if he could find the right one."

Michael said, "I wonder who else he might have called up by mistake."

Dad remarked, "I'm glad we don't have to pay that phone bill."

By now, Norman was singing "Oh, Susannah" to Fluffy.

"Get off the phone," said Dad.

Norman said goodnight and hung up.

Finally Dr. Sparks called. "Stanley's next feeding went well," she reported. "He kept the sock down and burped all right. And he did his next trash pickup well, too." Mom and Norman told her about Fluffy's phone call.

"That's amazing," she said. "Matt's in charge

of that plant this evening. Maybe he went out to watch the broadcast from space and stopped to get something to eat on the way back. But this is exciting news about Fluffy learning a new behavior. And it solves a mystery. When I called home tonight, my husband said they'd been getting nuisance calls all evening with nobody talking. My home number's programmed into the speed dialing just like yours."

After they finished talking to Dr. Sparks, it was past the boys' bedtime. When Dad came in to say goodnight, Norman was in bed but Michael was standing by the window, looking up at the night sky.

"I was just thinking about Stanley being up there somewhere," said Michael. "I wonder where he is now."

Dad looked at his watch. "It's been three hours since their broadcast. It takes the shuttle an hour and a half to go around the world, so Stanley's already traveled around the world twice since we saw him tonight. Tomorrow maybe we can find out what continents and oceans they're flying over at what times of day. And remember, they fly through sixteen sunrises and sixteen sunsets every twenty-four hours. So Stanley's going through sixteen days and nights in one day."

Dad turned out the light. "Sleep tight," he said and went out.

Norman wondered aloud, "But Stanley eats every night. Is he going to get mixed up and eat sixteen times a day?"

"No," said Michael. "Dr. Sparks said the plants would eat on their regular schedule."

"I think Fluffy ate too early tonight," said Norman.

"I'm sure he's fine," replied Michael.

"But what if Stanley eats sixteen times a day?" continued Norman. "He'll grow so big that when the shuttle comes back to Earth, he won't be able to get out the door. He'll have to stay in the shuttle always. Unless they take it apart to let him out. And then he won't fit back in our room here when he comes home."

"Stop yapping," said Michael. "I'm not listening."

"He'll have to live in the garage," said Norman, "because that's the only door we've got that's big enough for him to get through. And we'll have to make the roof higher because he's too tall."

Michael fell asleep thinking of Stanley, grown to the size of Godzilla, rolling through the city on a giant skateboard, smashing the roofs of sock stores and feeding on the contents. Or maybe a factory would have to start making Godzilla-size socks to feed him and keep him from wrecking the city.

Chapter 20

Next morning the school was swarming with visitors. A television truck was parked outside. A reporter from the newspaper was going around asking questions and taking notes. The cafeteria was packed with children sitting on the floor.

Those who were going to ask questions sat in front. They clutched papers with their questions written on them. Michael kept repeating his silently in his mind, so he would not mess up when his turn came. He noticed Chad was moving his lips, practicing his question, too.

The phone line radio link was set up in front. Michael was surprised to see that it was a regular telephone receiver.

Mr. Leedy welcomed everyone. He warned that when a question was being asked the audience must be absolutely silent and still. Any noise would interfere with the radio transmission.

The teleconference started right on time. The Mission Commander appeared in the video projection on the wall and said, "Welcome to our classroom in space!"

The other crew members gathered around him. Each waved as he announced their names. He welcomed all the schools that were watching and especially four of the astronauts' old schools that they were going to take questions from today.

Mark Fortunato was first. The others got out of the way to give him room. There was no sign of Stanley.

"I'm really glad to be speaking to you at my old school today," Mark said. "I sat and studied at those desks where you sit now. I used to ride my bike around that neighborhood. I skateboarded on Oak Street with my friends. You know the good part where it slants downhill? And I dreamed of becoming an astronaut. Now let's have the first question."

A fourth-grade girl was ready at the phone. "My name is Ashleigh," she said, "and we want to know if a yo-yo will work in space."

Mark took a yo-yo out of his pocket. "I brought one along because I knew you were going to ask that, Ashleigh. And I've been practicing. Here goes." He threw the yo-yo out sideways on its string. It rolled right back to his hand.

He said, "You see it works just like on Earth, Ashleigh. Next question."

Chad stepped up. "My name is Chad, and my friend Michael and I want to know: Can you play basketball in microgravity?"

"That's an interesting question, Chad," replied Mark. "We brought along a hoop so we can try it." He pointed to a toy hoop mounted on the wall to the left. One of the crew out of sight of the camera tossed him a toy basketball. Mark threw it one-handed toward the net. The ball went in and stopped, not falling through.

"I'll try it with a little more force," said Mark. This time it went through, down to the unseen floor and back up again. Mark twirled himself around and dunked the ball from the bottom up. It kept going to the ceiling and glided down.

"We can slam dunk down or up," Mark added. "And we can do this, too." He pulled his knees up to his chest, and wrapped his arms around them. He gave himself a little push, somersaulted slowly in midair, and put the ball in the basket. Michael noticed the socks he was wearing were fudge ripple.

"Of course," said Mark, "in a basketball game in space, every player on both teams, even short people, could jump higher than the greatest players in the NBA on Earth. They'd have to be careful not to bump their heads on the ceiling. And once they've jumped, they might not come all the way back down. The game would be a lot slower. The rules would have to be changed for floating players." He chuckled. "Next question."

Chad asked, "Can you dribble the ball?"

"Okay, we'll try that." He threw the ball down to the floor, up to the ceiling, and off the side wall. It returned to him slowly.

"We can dribble in any direction. Next question."

Michael was next. His mouth was dry. His hands felt clammy. He was afraid his voice would shake, but it didn't.

"My name is Michael, and I want to know how the plantronaut is doing in space."

Suddenly, at the sound of Michael's voice, before Mark could answer, a leafy vine yanked the astronaut aside. A mass of leaves and vines filled the picture. Stanley was giving himself a closeup!

Michael exclaimed, "Hey, Stanley! How are you?"

They could hear Mark saying, "Stop that! Move over!"

But Stanley was apparently so glad to hear Michael that he would not budge. In the middle of the huge closeup picture of solid greenery, fingers appeared. They pried the vines apart just enough for the astronaut's face to peek through the leaves.

"As you can see, Michael," said Mark, "the plant has made itself right at home here in space. At first it had a little trouble getting used to weightlessness. But it's doing fine now.

"This is a very special plant," he added. "Wait. I'm getting leaves in my mouth. Let me get the plant out of the way here."

It wasn't clear at first what Mark was doing, but Stanley moved back. Then a fudge ripple sock appeared. Mark was dangling it in front of the plant and moving away. Stanley glided out of the picture, following the sock. They heard a loud "Schlurrrp!"

Everyone laughed. Mark reappeared. "That wasn't me," he said, grinning. "That noise is one of the special things about this plant. Plants help clean the air, so some kinds will be especially useful for that in future space travel. And for growing food in space, too. On this flight, we're experimenting with this plant performing some tasks. So far, it looks promising."

Across the miles from space, they heard a mighty "Burrrrp!" Everyone in the cafeteria burst out laughing.

Mark started laughing, too. "That wasn't me. Again," he said. "It's another special plant noise. We better go on to the next question."

Mr. Leedy stepped up to the front and put a finger to his lips, signaling everyone to be quiet so the next question could be transmitted. Most people were able to stop laughing, but a few had to go out in the hall. Some kids pressed their hands over their mouths to keep their giggles in.

Mark answered the rest of the questions and explained some scientific principles of how things work in space. For Michael most of this went by in a blur because he was watching the sides of the picture to see if he could catch another glimpse of Stanley. But no vines poked in.

A voice from Mission Control in Houston announced that there was one minute left before switching to the next school waiting to ask questions. Mark quickly finished what he was explaining.

The next astronaut came on and began answering questions from her old school.

Chapter 21

After the teleconference, Mom and Dad came to find Michael.

"You did a wonderful job asking your question," said Dad. "I was proud of you."

"Me, too," said Mom. "You sounded calm and collected."

"I was nervous," Michael said.

"Well, it didn't show," said Dad. "But I was afraid there for a minute that Stanley was going to hog the whole teleconference. Thank goodness that astronaut knew how to get him to behave."

"Yes," added Mom. "He really knows how to handle Stanley."

Dad and Mom went on down the hall to stop in at Norman's room before going back to work. Michael thought about how he had always been the only one who knew how to handle Stanley.

Now Mark Fortunato could do it. And Dr. Sparks, too. Michael was surprised to find himself feeling a little jealous.

In that afternoon's phone report, Dr. Sparks said Stanley had settled down nicely after Mark had distracted him with the sock. He was back to doing his tasks pretty well.

She was running Fluffy through the same tasks on the same schedule. So when Stanley had trouble with the latch on the trash bin, she worked it out with Fluffy and sent word to Mark about how to solve the problem.

Michael asked, "When do you think our plants can come home?"

"About a week after the landing," she said. "Stanley will have to get used to not being weightless any more. And I'll do measurements and tests on both plants to compare them and see if eight days in space has had any effects on Stanley."

Norman asked, "What do you mean effects? Like special effects?"

"No, I mean changes. I need to find out if Stanley is different in any way than before he went to space."

That night Mom told Dad, "Two more weeks of plant vacation. I'm really enjoying this plant-free lifestyle. Except for Norman's popcorn explosion, we haven't had any messy disasters or middle-of-the-night uproars while they've been away."

"Let's enjoy it while we can," replied Dad. "This quiet time will be gone before we know it."

In the boys' room, as they were going to sleep, Norman said, "Do you think when Stanley gets back he'll glow in the dark?"

"No," said Michael. "When astronauts get back, they don't glow in the dark. So Stanley won't either. Quit worrying."

Norman went on, "But in comic books sometimes things like that happen."

"Real life is not like comic books," said Michael.

"Are you sure?" asked Norman.

"Yes."

Norman thought about that for a while. Then he said, "Have you ever seen a picture of an astronaut in the dark?"

"This is silly," replied Michael.

Norman thought some more.

"But if Stanley does glow in the dark," he continued, "he can be a nightlight for us. A really big nightlight."

"Great," said Michael, giving up. "Then we can read in bed after Mom and Dad make us turn out our lights."

"Cool," replied Norman.

Chapter 22

For the first mock space flight, the whole school assembled in the gym. Michael's class had practiced and was ready to go. As they marched single-file through the crowd, the other children waved and cheered.

Kimberly Offenberg carried a three-ring notebook with lists of everything they were to do. The others carried lists of their own duties.

They entered the mock-up shuttle and took their places. Mission Control started the countdown on the PA.

Just for fun Mr. Jones had attached a big bunch of sparklers in the back of the mock-up to stand in for rocket engines. He had brought three pails of water and a fire extinguisher, as he put it, "to be on the safe side." He turned down the lights so the sparklers would look more exciting.

He told Mr. Leedy, "You hold the extinguisher while I fire up the sparklers. We don't want to take any chances."

The principal picked up the extinguisher. "This is a new model I've never seen before," he observed. "Wait till I read the directions."

But the crowd had joined in yelling the countdown, making so much noise that Mr. Jones did not hear him clearly.

"Zero!" roared the crowd. Mr. Jones quickly lit the sparklers. They sputtered into a cascade of flying lights. The kids cheered and whistled. Over the deafening noise the voice from Mission Control shouted over the PA, "We have lift-off!"

Mr. Leedy, still trying to read the long directions in tiny letters in the dim light, accidentally turned on the extinguisher. A burst of foam spewed over the floor and kept coming. The first couple of rows of children shrieked and hopped out of the way. The pails of water got kicked over in the confusion.

"Turn it off!" yelled Mr. Jones.

"I'm trying," yelled Mr. Leedy, "but you better do it. I didn't get to read all the directions."

Mr. Jones grabbed the extinguisher from him and tried to turn it off. But the foam kept erupting. "It's stuck!" he exclaimed.

By now the whole crowd was roaring with laughter. The kids in front were trying to stay out of the way of the foam. The sparklers began fizzling out.

Inside the Spacelab, Michael was tending to some seedlings. He pushed two of the walls on wheels apart just enough to peek out.

He said into the nearest baby monitor, "Commander, this is Spacelab. Somebody's spraying foam in the gym. I don't know what they're doing out there." He paused and realized he had just stepped into a puddle. He continued, "And water's coming in under the wall."

Kim's voice replied calmly, "We're up in space. We have to keep going with our mission."

"Okay," said Michael. "I read you loud and clear." Then he went back to peeking out at the scene outside the walls.

Mr. Leedy was shouting to Mr. Jones, "Take that extinguisher outside!" Gesturing with his arms, he tried to part a path to the door through the mob.

Mr. Jones moved quickly, but he had to keep aiming the foam at the floor in front of him to keep from getting it on the children. He slipped and slid along. Two tall sixth-grade boys grabbed him under the arms to keep him from falling. The three of them skidded together and landed in a heap. The foam went up and sideways, covering a larger area.

Mr. Leedy shouted to Mr. Jones, "Is this a toxic chemical?"

"No!" yelled the custodian. He and the two sixth-graders were trying to get up off the floor and were not succeeding.

A third-grade girl ran up to Mr. Leedy and said, "That's just like the extinguisher my dad used for fake snow for my birthday party last summer. It's okay to play in."

"Thank you for telling me that," Mr. Leedy replied. Over the uproar he yelled, "Don't worry, everybody! This foam is perfectly harmless!"

Only the nearest kids heard him, but that was all it took for them to start sliding through the foam. The heap of it next to Mr. Jones was mushrooming fast. Somebody jumped into it. Splat! Gobs of foam went flying. More joined in, laughing and sliding. Others circled around, egging them on.

Mr. Leedy, Mr. Jones, and all the teachers yelled at them to stop, but this went unheard or unheeded in the uproar. Mr. Leedy realized he needed a mike fast. He burst into the crew deck, stepped up on the ladder, and stuck his head up through the hole in the flight deck floor.

"I need to make an announcement!" he said.

But Kimberly Offenberg was taking her mission commander duties very seriously. She apparently thought this was some kind of trick test of her astronaut knowledge. She replied, "But we're up in space, a hundred and sixty miles above Earth. Nobody can get in from outside. To talk to us you have to go through Mission Control in the office."

Mr. Leedy said sternly, "I'm a Klingon stopping in for a space visit. I just beamed myself up. Hand me that mike."

Kimberly handed it over. He turned up the volume.

His voice boomed over the gym, "Hold it, everybody! Don't move! Stop right where you are!"

Everybody stood still except one kid who had started a long slide just before Mr. Leedy spoke. He couldn't stop until he ran into a wall.

"I want silence," commanded Mr. Leedy in a voice-of-doom tone. "Complete silence!" The crowd shut up.

With order restored, the teachers rounded up their classes and marched them back to their rooms, tracking foam down the hall.

As the gym cleared out, Mr. Jones crawled to a unfoamed spot where he could stand up.

"What a mess!" he said.

"How do we clean this up?" asked Mr. Leedy.

Mr. Jones replied, "Probably shovel it into trash cans. Unless it evaporates. How about getting the ringleaders in here to help?"

"Excellent idea," agreed Mr. Leedy.

* * *

With no further uproar in the gym, Mrs. Black's class completed their mission and landed the imaginary shuttle safely. Mrs. Black told them they had done an excellent job. As they trooped out, another class came in to take off.

Back in their room, after they talked about their flight, Mrs. Black had them write in their journals about it.

Michael was having trouble keeping his mind on his writing. He kept wondering how Stanley was doing. The room was quiet except for the shuffling of feet under desks, the whirr of the pencil sharpener, and an occasional snuffle from Jason, who had a cold.

Michael's nose noticed that a delicious smell had wafted down the hall from the cafeteria and into their open door. He poked Brad and silently said "Pizza." Brad nodded and smiled. Michael looked at the clock. It was T minus ten minutes to lunch and counting.

Meanwhile, out in space, Mark Fortunato asked another astronaut, "Did you just see something very small float by?"

"No. Where?"

"There it is again! It's a bug!" Mark grabbed for it but missed it.

128

His crewmate asked, "How could it have gotten in here?"

"Not from outer space," replied Mark, laughing. "Remember that uninvited mosquito that sneaked into a shuttle a few years ago?"

"Yeah, that was quite a surprise for the crew."

Mark added, "Being up in space must have been an even bigger surprise for the mosquito. There's the bug again! I caught it! Find something to put it in."

"I've seen bugs like this before," said his crewmate. "They eat other bugs that damage plants. I ordered some of these for my garden last year from an ad in a magazine."

After he put the bug away, Mark looked around.

"Did you see my notebook?" he asked. "I left it right here when I turned around to catch the bug."

"You must have knocked it with your elbow and it floated away." They looked all over. No notebook.

"It has to be here somewhere," said Mark. "But it isn't."

Chapter 23

While they searched, Stanley glided by. He tried to pull off one of Mark's socks, but Mark gently pushed the vine away.

They finally found the notebook in the trash bin, where Stanley had put it. They also found some other things that didn't belong in there.

Mark said, "The plant must have grabbed this other stuff in between its pickup exercises. It's getting too eager about doing its job! We'll have to keep a closer eye on it."

Behind their backs, as they took lost objects from the trash bin and put them away, Stanley floated toward one of the holes in the ceiling that led to the flight deck above.

As Mark turned around, he glimpsed just the tip of a vine disappearing through the hole.

"Hey, come back here!" he called. He began pulling himself toward the hole to get the plant.

But before he got there, they heard the mission commander yell from the deck above, "Get that plant out of the pilot's seat!"

After that Stanley had to spend more of his spare time snugly wrapped up in his specially made sleep restraint.

The next morning at breakfast, Dad was reading the newspaper.

"Listen to this!" he exclaimed. "On the shuttle yesterday they found a bug that wasn't supposed to be there. Apparently it rode in on something that went into the shuttle. Like that mosquito that got on a flight a few years ago."

Michael stopped chewing his Super Gooper Bunch-O-Crunch to ask, "What kind of bug was it?"

"It doesn't say," replied Dad.

Michael said with his mouth full, "I wonder."

"What?" asked Dad.

"No, it couldn't be," said Michael. He went on crunching.

Mom asked, "Couldn't be what?"

"One of our bugs," he said, "that could have been hiding somewhere on Stanley."

"No," she agreed. "It couldn't be."

*　　*　　*

131

On landing day, Mr. Leedy announced on the PA that the radio news reported that the orbiter had come down safely. Cheers went up throughout the school.

That evening the family watched the events on the TV news. When they saw the landing gears hit the runway, Michael yelled, "Touchdown!"

"It's not a football game," said Norman.

Michael replied, "That's what space people say when the orbiter touches down on the ground. Didn't you see that fact in the hall at school?"

"Oh," said Norman.

"They only get one chance to land," said Michael. "They can't pull up and come back around to try it again."

Mom said, "I'm glad they made it all right."

Norman began hopping around the living room, shouting, "The plants are coming home! The plants are coming home!"

"It won't be long," said Dad.

Dr. Sparks called to report that Stanley was fine, but lying down a lot.

"What's wrong with him?" asked Michael. This was alarming news.

"He's just resting," Dr. Sparks assured him. "When people return after being weightless in space, Earth's gravity makes them feel as if they weigh four hundred pounds. And they've lost some muscle strength. Stanley's going through the same thing. He feels very heavy. His vines are weaker than usual. And he's still a little wobbly."

"When will he be okay?" Michael asked.

"Soon. Every couple of hours, Matt and I get him up on his skateboard and walk him around. We put his vines over our shoulders for support."

"Are you sure he'll be all right?" asked Michael.

"I'm positive," replied Dr. Sparks. "Once he gets used to not being weightless, he'll be the same as ever. Just like Fluffy, who stayed on Earth. No changes. Except, of course, that now they're both highly trained trash picker-uppers. That should come in handy when they get home."

Mom, who was on the other phone, said, "I don't think we'll have them do that. Having them just standing around eating socks is enough."

Chapter 24

To prepare a special treat for Stanley's return, Michael wore the same pair of fudge ripple socks for three days straight. He thought this would make them especially delicious.

Norman complained about the smell when Michael took the socks off at night. Michael ignored him.

At the end of the week, Dr. Sparks had finished all the tests comparing Fluffy and Stanley.

"Is Stanley back to acting regular?" Michael asked her.

"Almost," she replied. "He's standing up all the time. His vines are stronger. But he's still just a little confused. In space, with a tug or shove, he could push off sideways or upside down. Of course, he can't do that anymore. Now it takes more force for him to move himself around.

Sometimes he uses not enough or too much. But he'll get that straightened out in a few days, I'm sure."

The plants were coming home in a truck on Saturday. Norman and Bob made a long sign on Bob's computer that said: "Welcome Home Fluffy and Stanley, Plantronauts from Space. We Missed You. Fudge Ripple for Supper Tonight." The sign was so long that they had to cut it up in four pieces to hang it on the wall.

Mrs. Smith gave Norman some balloons to blow up. "They say 'Happy Birthday' on them," she said, "but you can turn that part around so it doesn't show."

On the big day, Norman spent the afternoon looking out the front window, watching for the truck. Bob kept him company for a while, but then he got bored and went home.

Michael went outside to watch for the truck. As he stood on the sidewalk, he noticed that Mrs. Smith had changed the costume on her goose. It was wearing a green plant outfit, with leaves and vines.

About four o'clock the truck pulled up. Matt opened the back and put down the ramp. The boys climbed in to roll their plants down.

Norman flung his arms around Fluffy. His plant flung its vines around him. Michael put an arm around Stanley.

"I'm glad you're home," he said. Stanley looked fine.

Mom and Dad invited Matt and the driver in for a meal. Mrs. Smith came over, bringing a cake with leaves and vines on it made of green frosting. Bob saw her going by with the cake and followed her in.

As they sat around the dining room table, Matt said, "I'm going to miss Fluffy. Would you be willing to sell him?"

"How much?" asked Mom.

"Never!" said Norman. "He's my friend!"

Matt smiled, "I know what you mean. He was fun to work with in the lab. And he's probably the only plant in the world that makes phone calls!"

That night, the plants were back in their usual places, next to the boys' beds. Michael was sprawled on his bed, reading. Norman came in, closed the door, and turned out all the lights.

Michael squawked, "What do you think you're doing?"

"I want to see if Stanley will glow in the dark."

"I told you he wouldn't!"

Norman replied, "I'm checking just in case."

Michael reached for the nearest lamp and switched it on.

"He's not glowing!" he yelled.

"Maybe if we wait in the dark a while, he might," Norman suggested.

"Okay, then you stay awake all night and watch him." Michael went back to his book.

At bedtime, the boys laid out the plants' socks meals on the floor—dirty for Stanley, clean for Fluffy. Things were back to normal.

While Norman was in the bathroom, Michael went to the kitchen and got a small flashlight. He stuck it in the dirt in Stanley's pot, with the bulb end pointed up. Then he turned out the lights and crawled into bed.

Norman returned.

"Those dirty socks really stink!" he complained.

"Then hold your nose," said Michael.

After Mom and Dad came in to say goodnight, the boys lay in the dark, with just a little light coming in from the hall.

"I can still smell those stinky socks all the way over here," whined Norman.

Michael did not reply. He wanted to make Norman think he was already asleep. He waited a while longer. Then he reached in among Stanley's leaves and switched on the flashlight.

Norman went "Eeeeek" and shot out of bed.

"He's glowing!" he squealed. "Stanley's glowing! Wake up! Look! Look! He's glowing!"

Michael switched off the flashlight.

"He's not glowing," said Michael. "You must have been dreaming."

"I wasn't asleep."

"Go back to bed," said Michael.

"But I saw it," said Norman, getting suspicious. He turned on a light and looked closely at Stanley. He pulled out the flashlight.

"Aha!" he exclaimed.

"Well," said Michael, "you said you wanted him to glow."

Dad and Mom rushed in to see what was the matter.

Norman explained in his whiniest tone of voice.

"Stop teasing your brother," Dad told Michael. "Both of you settle down and go to sleep."

But Norman had kept the flashlight. He stuck it in Fluffy's pot and turned it on.

The boys both started laughing and couldn't stop. Dad had to come in two more times to tell them to shut up and go to sleep.

After they finally fell asleep, Stanley reached over and pulled Michael's blanket up to his chin. Fluffy patted Norman on the head.

Late that night the plants ate their meals. Stanley kept poking at his socks, as if trying to get them to play. He had gotten used to fishing for socks that were floating in space, not ones lying still on the floor. The plants schlurped and burped, and Fluffy said, "Ex."

After dinner they began moving on their skateboards. Trying to pull himself along with a vine,

Stanley tugged gently. That would be enough to get him moving in space, but not on Earth. Trying again, he yanked too hard. That sent him zooming across the room. He slammed into Michael's bureau. Slowly he worked his way into the hall, banging into walls and furniture here and there along the way.

Fluffy followed without bumping into anything. He dragged himself to the closet by the front door where the boys' remote-control trucks were kept. Fluffy picked up the controls and handed one to Stanley. Each plant held onto a truck with a vine and began towing himself around.

They raced up and down the hall for a while. Then they were ready to do something else. They had not picked up and put away any trash yet that day. So they began feeling around for things to pick up.

In the living room Stanley picked up magazines and knickknacks from the coffee table. He could not find a trash bin, so he tucked them under the couch cushions.

In the kitchen Fluffy found some real trash. A bulging black plastic bag stood by the back door, ready to be carried out to a garbage can by the garage. He jerked the top, and it came open.

Inside he found vegetable peelings, empty milk cartons and cereal boxes, wet paper towels, food

139

scraps from dinner, and crumpled paper napkins smeared with food goo.

To complete his task, Fluffy needed something like the trash bin he had trained with—something that had a handle to open and close.

He went to work, using his excellent trash-training experience. Piece by piece, Fluffy neatly put all the garbage into the refrigerator.